MW01608980

The Beginning

Of

A New Dawn

Roger Henri Trepanier

© 2015

This book is dedicated to all the women of this world who aspired to and fulfilled the oldest and most honorable profession on earth, which is to be a wife and mother!

"Charm is deceitful and beauty is vain, but a woman who fears the Lord, she shall be praised."

Proverbs 31:30

**Titles available from Roger Henri Trepanier in
The Truth Seeker's Library™ series:**

God Did Not Create Human Beings To Die... But To Live On...
Eternally!

Finding Comfort And Encouragement In The Promises Of God In
The Last Days

How We Know For Sure That We Are Living In The Last Days!

Have You Ever Wondered What Happens After Death?

An Introduction To The New World That Is Coming On The Earth

Deeper Truths Of The Christian Life

Evangelism As God Intended

**Titles available from Roger Henri Trepanier in
The Practical Helps Library™ series:**

Learning to Overcome The Perplexities Of This Present Life

So, I Hear You Want To Work With Seniors?

Preface

This is the author's first book in "The Christian Fiction Library™" series. It is hoped that many will enjoy this love story within a love story, which has been a real pleasure to write. In fact, on many days I did not want to stop, even for meals, as the words were flowing freely.

Since the author is also a Christian counselor of many years, there are many aspects of that counseling experience which has been incorporated into the story and it is hoped will be helpful to many.

And as can be expected in a work of fiction, the characters and events portrayed in this book are fictitious. Any similarities to real persons, living or dead, are purely coincidental, and were not the intent of the author.

Trusting all will enjoy the story!

Roger Henri Trepanier

CONTENTS

Page

Preface

THE NEXT BOOK

"Behold, children are a gift of the Lord,

the fruit of the womb is a reward."

Psalm 127:3

Chapter One

/ Born with a silver spoon in her mouth

If ever there was a child born with a silver spoon in her mouth, it was Dawn. Not only was she a healthy 7 lbs at birth, but she had beautiful blond hair and sky blue eyes, which was enough to make one look twice, even at this stage of her life. Her parents, Ben and Sarah, had anticipated this moment for almost nine months, Dawn being the first offspring of a couple in love. They had been married for almost two years, having been sweethearts since their freshman year in college, where they met. Now Dawn was resting comfortably in her mother's arms, barely a day old. Both sets of proud grandparents have arrived, along with a host of other family, friends, and even neighbors, since Ben's father, Jim had been raised in the area and was very well known. Hospital staff is having a hard time maintaining the hospital rule of only four visitors in the room at any one time.

Ben is by Sarah's hospital bed beaming from ear to ear. On the table nearby is a beautiful flower arrangement to Sarah from Ben, with a large box of chocolates. Ben will have to hold off on that box of cigars he had also purchased, not knowing if the child was to be a boy or a girl. But a girl it was and Ben's heart was still overflowing with thankfulness for what God had provided them. Although Ben believed, like so many, that there was a God, yet no one ever told him that he could know Him personally. To Ben, God was just the 'Big Guy Upstairs,' as he was in the habit of calling Him. Sarah's faith did not go much deeper. Being a woman, she had more refined spiritual sensitivities than her husband and yearned for something more than just believing that there was a Creator of all the beauty she saw in nature around where they lived.

11

When Sarah had started having her labor pains early the previous morning, Ben did not waste any time in driving her to the nearest hospital in the northwest of the city, which was twenty miles from their resort. His father, who had retired at forty-five, having made his fortune in real estate by then, had turned the controlling share of the resort over to Ben, who had graduated from college with a degree in Hotel and Resort Management, the spring before their summer marriage. Sarah had graduated with a degree in nursing, which was a perfect match for the Twin Peaks Resort, Golf, and RV Park, which they now partly owned and managed.

The resort owned 300 acres of property semi-circle around Crystal lake, about a mile wide by two miles long, which was fed by a year round river from two opposing sets of glacial mountains, less than a mile away and running north and south. The state owned the first sixty feet around the lake, which had been designated for public access. The resort owned 160 units on the lake, eighty one bedroom units, sixty two bedroom units, and forty three bedroom units going from west to east. The 300 spot RV park ran the full length behind the units, with a paved road owned by the resort separating the two areas. There was a public beach across from units, which was just over a 1000 feet from the turnoff from the four lane Interstate Highway nearby, which continued on into the next state, going through a pass between the two sets of mountains. The state had also built a small hydroelectric dam at the east end of the lake to control the water at a constant level, so there would never be any flooding, and also to provide electricity which was being fed in the state electric grid.

About 1000 feet from the Interstate turnoff, and before reaching the lake, there was a road going west which lead to the eight bedroom house, sitting on ten acres of property, which had a ten foot high wall all around, which was where Ben and Sarah lived. This is where Ben's parents, Jim and Dot, had lived before they semi-retired and moved to another state. On the same road coming from the Interstate and running north, and just before arriving at the lake, there was a resort office, a restaurant, a store, and a small clinic managed by Sarah. On the other side of the Interstate was an 18 hole executive golf course, with a clubhouse, also owned by the resort, with the two areas being connected by an overpass over the highway, with a separate lane for motorized golf carts. There were many year round residents who stayed in the RV park, or who rented a unit from the resort. Ben and Sarah oversaw a staff of over ninety employees, which kept them busy.

Ben has just been told by the doctor that he can take Sarah home the next morning, barely thirty-six hours after she gave birth, as both Sarah and child have been examined and found to be in excellent health. So Dawn's young life is seen to start on the best of footings – as used by the standards of this world - she was wanted, had parents who loved each other, were well-off financially, and she was a healthy baby. Her parents would be there to provide whatever their little girl would ever need or want. Maybe that spoon was of gold, and not silver!

"Train up a child in the way he should go, even when he is old he will not depart from it."

Proverbs 22:6

Chapter Two

/ Even silver tarnishes

Even the flattest of roads eventually encounter a bump or two. After all, this is life on earth and not Heaven. And fairy tales are only the product of someone's imagination. Then too, good beginnings do not automatically mean a good ending. Life is unknowable, which is why God says to the human race, "Come now, you who say, "Today or tomorrow we will go to such and such a city, and spend a year there and engage in business and make a profit." Yet you do not know what your life will be like tomorrow. You are just a vapor that appears for a little while and then vanishes away. Instead, you ought to say, "If the Lord wills, we will live and also do this or that." But as it is, you boast in your arrogance; all such boasting is evil." So although Dawn started life here on earth with loving parents, who were well to do financially, she still faced some challenges growing up.

Two years after Dawn was born, Ben and Sarah added a pair of identical twins to their family, Amy and Zoe. As anyone knows who has ever grown up with a set of identical twins, they act as one. That is to say, they not only dress alike, but they also look alike, think alike, and act in similar ways. As Dawn was to find out, to her consternation, the twins would mostly keep to themselves, almost seeing her as an outsider. As Dawn grew older, she expected to have sisters to play with, but instead found herself being shunned by the twins. She ended up as if she had been an only child in her family. After the twins had been born, the doctors had found a tumor in Sarah's uterus, which turned out to be cancerous. With the approval of both Ben and Sarah, her doctor had performed a hysterectomy, which meant that she would not be able to have any more children, at least by natural means. And Ben's dream of having a boy to one day be involved with him in the resort, slowly faded as some distant memory, as the days passed into months and then into years.

Being an attractive young girl with blond hair and clear blue eyes seemed to compensate for Dawn's lack of sibling companionship as she grew older. She could not help but notice that wherever she went, heads would turn for a second look. And again, as any attractive woman knows, beauty can be a bonus or a curse, depending on how one handles that gift. For one thing, it did not take Dawn long to find out that feminine beauty has a way of drawing boys. Then add the fact that she inherited her mother's figure, which was further enhanced by spending much time in the water and in the sun, and the result could be spelled 'dynamite.' This was the bonus part of her external appearance.

The curse was that although Dawn could attract almost any boy at will, this meant for a lot of choices, which further meant wanting to sample many, but settling for none. In other words, without Dawn being fully aware, she found herself growing shallow as she grew older. This shallowness was the result of three forces acting at once upon her. On the one hand, many suitors meant constantly thinking that she should not grow a relationship just now, in case the next one would be her prince charming. Although Dawn had dreamt of marriage and children for as long as she could remember, yet in her teen years it looked like that dream would never be realized.

The second force which tended to make Dawn shallow as she grew into a young woman was the fact that character is usually developed best in adversity. To Dawn, that was a foreign word. Since being born, all she needed was provided for her. She did not grow up with crooked teeth, for when she required braces, her parents could afford those dental bills, which meant she had near perfect teeth. So whereas many kids show missing teeth when they smile, this was a problem that was far from touching Dawn. Similarly with her complexion, she did not have to think twice about pimples and acne, since being well-off financially meant that her parents could afford a dermatologist, should one ever be needed. But in Dawn's case, it was not. She had good nutrition, since her mom was a nurse and knew more than the average mom in that area. Also, Dawn exuded confidence, which was another trait which she inherited from her parents, so that this too helped her complexion stay clear, as she was not beset with the anxiety that so often accompanies the teen years. And so any problem Dawn ever faced was but a challenge for her college-educated parents to face and meet for her. Ben and Sarah tried to shield her from the adversities of life, which they meant for good, but which was not always helpful.

The third force and no doubt the most important, although she, and her parents, did not know it at the time, was that Dawn was growing up lopsided. They thought - as do all humans who take God off the shelf on Sundays, or only when they sense a need for someone greater than themselves - that life could be lived on the physical, emotional, social, and psychological plane, without giving much thought to the spiritual component of life, and even less to an afterlife. What this meant for Dawn, as she grew older, same as it means for all humans who think this way, is that one goes through life thinking that one can make it on one's own, without God. In other words, even though God is The One Who designed us and brought us into being, and also has the owner's manual for living on earth, yet too many think that once born we can go our own way without Him, much like a Pinocchio. Ben and Sarah had not trained up Dawn in the way that she should go, meaning in a way which has God in mind. And so they were all about to find out the consequence of that.

"Do not be deceived, God is not mocked; for whatever a man sows, this he will also reap."

Galatians 6:7

Chapter Three

/ A rose has thorns

One thing which Dawn had in common with every other female is the God-given drive to procreate after one's kind, which God put in His blueprint for the whole of the human race and for all of his creatures on earth. Of course, under normal circumstances, this requires the female to be on the lookout for the best available male, and not to settle for just any offering, of which these are a dime a dozen. In Dawn's case, the task was somewhat easier due to the sheer number of candidates she was constantly being faced with. Here the challenge for her, as is true of every young woman growing up, is to eventually settle down with some measure of dignity left. In some ways, it is like playing Monopoly and trying to make it to 'Go' with some money left.

And there is another downside here, which is that boys tend to mature at least three years behind the females, until they catch up around the age of twenty-five. What this means is that whereas the female might be thinking of marriage and children by the time she reaches her mid to late teens, the male is only thinking of satisfying his sex drive, which is most often than not in overdrive, and even more so in a society where there is so much flesh shown that one would think the clothing industry has gone out of business! So whenever Dawn would date, which was often after she reached sixteen - since that was when her parents had said she could - she found herself fighting off hands which had a habit of trying to get into places where they had not been invited.

Another problem which Dawn soon discovered, which she was not aware of before, is that there is no doubt a connection between one's mouth and one's sex organs. What is meant here is that when Dawn started letting boys kiss her, she also noticed that her breasts and vaginal area were affected, not knowing that God had designed her in such a way that blood would flow to those areas in preparation for the sexual act to follow. And of course, the same would have been occurring in the boy she would have been kissing, namely his genitals would be becoming engorged with blood. The one problem here though, which those who do not yet know God discard with impunity, is that God meant for this act to occur within the confines of marriage, between a man and a woman who love each other, and who are ready for what may result, which is a pregnancy. That is why many Christian parents advise their kids not to start kissing until they had found the one they are ready to settle down with in marriage. In some cultures today, the Amish being one example, this rule is still in practice.

What Dawn was also to discover, which would affect her for the rest of her life on earth, was that we cannot always control ourselves once our lust takes over. In other words, when kissing starts, it is hard to then start drawing the red lines in the sand. Either one has standards that one will not go beyond, or else one will just let the flow of emotions of the moment take over. And unfortunately for Dawn, this is what happened one Saturday night in late April. She had been dating Dave for three months. On this particular Saturday, Ben had allowed Dave to take his daughter over the mountains to the next state for an afternoon concert and then he was to return her home by midnight. As so often happens in life, events occur which we had not planned for. So after the concert, Dave suggested to Dawn that they stop for an evening meal at a well-known restaurant and then quickly take in a scenic spot he knew of on the other side of the Twin Peaks Mountains.

There are three things Dawn was to discover that night, which she had not given much thought to before, but which was to have far reaching consequences for her life. One is that music excites certain emotions, which play a part in one's sexual arousal. That is why many parents have tried over the years to control the type of music that their kids listen to, being in remembrance of the days of Elvis and what effect his music had on a whole generation. The second is that an evening meal with a male in a restaurant can also an effect on one's sexual arousal. Just looking into that face at close range for an hour or more, and especially if one already likes the person, can bring one to sexual arousal. Then that slow dance before they had their dessert, while Dawn and Dave's bodies pressed together to a rhythm, also did not do anything to lessen the sexual tension between them.

And so when Dave brought Dawn to that scenic spot in the mountains to pass an evening together looking at the moon and stars, and although neither one had planned it, yet when Dave leaned over and kissed Dawn, it was as if gasoline was flowing through their veins and igniting their skin at every point. That one kiss was the match that was needed to cause the flames to ignite. Then that one kiss led to a prolonged one which then fully aroused both of them, with the result that neither one of them wanted to apply the brakes to a situation that was leading both of them past the point of no return. As a first consequence, this turned out to be the night Dawn lost her virginity, which when lost can never be regained.

What Dawn was also not aware of, but soon learned, is that sex is pleasurable. And once engaged in, one wants to repeat the act. In other words, once Dawn had discovered the level of arousal that is achieved in this act of intimacy, then she could never just be satisfied with just leaving it at a kiss from then on. As a result, her and Dave found themselves engaging in the sexual act whenever they were alone together, even finding themselves lying to their close friends and especially to their parents, just to be together. Dawn somehow convinced herself that it was okay because she was sure she loved Dave, and he was more than likely the man she was going to marry. Little did she know Dave, and as it turned out, herself.

As too often happens in such situations, Dawn found herself in a situation she knew might come, but which she was not prepared for. One morning she woke up experiencing morning sickness, and after visiting the doctor, her worst fear was confirmed. She was now pregnant. But how could this be? She knew she was on the pill, so how could this have happened? Only when she visited a second doctor to confirm her predicament did Dawn find out that in a small percentage of cases one can still somehow get pregnant while on the pill. In other words, like every invention of man, nothing is fully guaranteed to work one hundred percent of the time.

And now Dawn was suddenly faced with quite a few real life dramas. What does she do now? Does she have the child? What is Dave going to say when she tells him? What does she say to her parents, who are sure to be disappointed with her? How does she tell this to her friends? If she decides to keep the child, does she drop out of school, being almost finished her senior year? And could she even go to school pregnant? She had always wanted to be married and have children, but not this way, with the children coming first. So many thoughts and questions now flooded her mind. It was as if she had grown a year in the space of one day, beginning with the second doctor having confirmed that she indeed was five weeks pregnant. Decisions needed to be made, and quick.

"…Behold, you have sinned against the Lord, and be sure your sin will find you out."

Numbers 32:23

Chapter Four

/ Facing the music

The first person Dawn had to tell, as soon as she could, was Dave. After all, she knew he was the father-to-be. Her and Dave had now been going out together for almost five months, having met in chemistry class, but having noticed each other a long time before that. Dave was the star quarterback on the high school football team, who, as often turns out in such situations, had been offered a football scholarship at a prestigious state college that coming fall. So just about every girl in school wanted him for a boyfriend, not just Dawn. And then Dawn for her part was one of the cheerleaders for the team, and with her blond hair and shapely figure, Dave had noticed her a long time before they actually started dating. But although externals may attract one to the other, it is the heart which must speak for the relationship to be a binding one. And unfortunately for Dawn, she was to discover that their hearts had not been engaged as much as she wished under her present circumstance.

Dave had driven in from the city to the resort as soon as he could make it, after sensing the urgency in Dawn's call to him that afternoon. They were now in his car, and as destiny would have it, and going to that scenic place over the mountains, where he had first been intimate with Dawn. Not a word had been said between them for the two hour drive, but as soon as they parked, Dawn turned to Dave and just came out with it, letting him know that she was pregnant. Dave just sat there dumbstruck at first, with a million thoughts clamoring for attention. Finally, Dawn asked him the question that was foremost on her mind, asking Dave point blank what he planned to do, since he was the father. Tears of sheer disappointment slowly started to fill Dawn's eyes as she heard Dave talk about his attending college that fall on his football scholarship and what his plans were for the future, which became clear in the telling that it did not include Dawn and a child. Dave was an only child, his father being an investment banker and his mother a doctor, specializing in obstetrics. From listening to Dave talk on and on, Dawn gathered that his parents had great expectations for their son, which did not include her.

Before they ended their conversation that late afternoon, reality had set in for Dawn. She now knew that Dave was not going to marry her, so from that perspective, what was the sense of carrying on the relationship? She was sure that she would not need his financial support; so on the way back to the Twin Peaks Resort, Dawn told Dave that she wanted to end the relationship, which Dave was glad to hear, although he did not tell Dawn. She then told him that they should still stay in touch, so that she could let him know when she had the baby, for she thought that as the father, he would take an interest in the child-to-be. Little did Dawn know then about this guy Dave, for the reality she would later come to see is that this was the last time she would ever see Dave.

When Dave dropped Dawn off at home in what was now early evening, she had decided that she had enough bad news to digest for one day and would hold off telling her parents until another day. However, sometimes events have a way of taking a life of their own, and when Dave dropped Dawn off at the house, he did not walk her to the door, as he normally did, nor did he hug her or kiss her. All this seemed strange to Sarah who was observing all this from a window in the living room of the house. So after Dawn had come in, and as can be expected, had gone directly to her bedroom, her mother followed her in and was sitting on her bed before Dawn could even close the door. The obvious question on Sarah's mind was: What had happened between her daughter and Dave? What Dawn was now thankful for, in a situation such as this, is having her mom as her best friend, so telling her the news, first of her and Dave breaking off their relationship, and then letting her know that she was pregnant, were not easy tasks, but at least bearable under her present circumstance. Sarah's reaction had been predicted by Dawn, as she just sat there, digesting it all before speaking, as she had done hundreds of times in the clinic, patiently listening to her patients before treating them. The fact was that Sarah was just numb with conflicting emotions, on the one hand, happy that she was going to have a grandchild, but on the other hand not happy to hear of her daughter being in this predicament. As a loving mother, she spoke with her heart first, putting her arms around Dawn, who was sitting on the bed beside her, letting her know, as she hugged her tight, that no matter what, she still loved her. Telling Dawn this was like opening and cleaning a badly infected wound, a lot of her suppressed emotions dating back to being told by the first doctor that she was pregnant now burst forth, like a breach in a dam. That day opened a new chapter in her relationship with her mother, where it was no longer just mother and daughter, but now her relationship had evolved into a woman to woman relationship, where Dawn was now being treated as an equal.

Both Dawn and Sarah finally decided that it was best to tell Ben right away, and so Sarah gave him a quick call on her cell phone to see where he was at that moment and what he was doing. When Sarah said it was an urgent matter, Ben was in Dawn's bedroom within fifteen minutes. Sarah spoke first and said that Dawn had news to share with him, for him to sit down. Dawn then proceeded to tell her father, whom she loved dearly and had never wanted to hurt him or disappoint him, that she was pregnant, that Dave was the father, and that her and Dave had broken up that afternoon. Ben, being a seasoned businessman of many years now, was just not prepared for the flood of emotions that came up over him when he heard this news, and just burst into tears as he sat there. Both Sarah and Dawn just looked at each other, not knowing what to say. Finally, Ben also spoke with his heart first and did exactly what Sarah had done earlier. He got up from his chair, walked over to the bed where Dawn was sitting and just held his daughter in his arms and told her that he loved her.

After that eventful day, things started to fall into place for Dawn. She had now made the crucial decision, in discussing the matter with her parents, that she was definitely going to keep the child. Both she and her parents did not believe in abortion, having long ago come to the conclusion, despite all they heard from the media, that life indeed did start at conception. Also, none of them wanted to give up the child for adoption, believing that it was not the child's fault that a mistake, albeit a sin in God's sight, had been committed. And so it was not up to strangers to raise this first child to enter their family. The decision had also been made that Dawn would continue to live at home, even after the child was born, with Ben being sure he could find some employment in the resort somewhere for her, if she wanted to work, while raising her child at home. Dawn was also glad to have graduated from high school that spring, so that meant not having to face schoolmates while she completed her pregnancy. And so, as Dawn waited with anticipation for the baby to come, she had a renewed sense that life was going to turn out well for her after all. What Dawn was thinking was true to a certain degree, but not in ways that Dawn envisioned them, as she was going to find out.

"A time to give birth and a time to die; a time to plant and a time to uproot what is planted… a time to weep and a time to laugh; a time to mourn and a time to dance."

Ecclesiastes. 3:2,4

Chapter Five

/ The timing could not have been worse

No one could have predicted what would befall Dawn's family, as she waited for her baby to arrive, which was any day now. During the last few months, Dawn had started to work in her father's office, which was located on the main floor of the house, for her parents thought it best that she not venture elsewhere on the property, especially since she needed to take fairly frequent naps. The pregnancy so far had been a normal one. Apart from the occasional morning sickness and the sudden craving for certain foods, Dawn was just like any other expecting mom-to-be.

When the police officer came to the door that Sunday evening, he found everyone at home and relaxing in the living room. That is, except Zoe, who had earlier gone out for a drive with her boyfriend. With the twins having recently turned sixteen, they were now also allowed to date, and this was where Zoe was. Out on a date with her new boyfriend. What Ben and Sarah had not liked about this relationship was that Zoe's boyfriend was only seventeen and had just got his driver's license, which came with a new sports car from his well-to-do parents. Ben was very much aware that a boy of seventeen is not a man, since those two years between sixteen and eighteen was when he remembers having gone through such a transformation, from being totally self-centered and arrogant as a teen to being a man at eighteen. And his own father had even noticed it and commented on it a few times.

In any case, when the policeman rang the doorbell that Sunday afternoon, it was to have a far-reaching effect for many years to come on Ben and Sarah's family. What the officer proceeded to say, after he had everyone sitting down, that is, Ben and Sarah, and Dawn and Amy, was that there had been an accident earlier that afternoon. Apparently the car Zoe was traveling in with her boyfriend went out of control and hit a rock cut in the mountain stretch of the Interstate Highway. Zoe was still alive when the ambulance got there, but died of her injuries on the way to the hospital. Her boyfriend had not been wearing a seatbelt and was killed instantly after having gone through the windshield upon impact. Now either Ben or Sarah was requested down at the city morgue to claim the body, although the authorities already had some idea as to who the deceased was based on the identification they found in a purse at the scene.

To Ben and Sarah especially, this news was as if an intruder had suddenly come into their home and had seized them by the throat, completely cutting off their breath. All while the officer spoke, it was as if both Ben and Sarah just sat there listening, but not wanting to hear, just wanting to be anywhere but there. As the news of Zoe's death suddenly hit their consciousness, they both burst into tears at the same time, fell to their knees on the carpet, and sobbed as if their eyes would run out of tears. The officer just sat there, really feeling sorry for what this couple was going through at the moment. As a seasoned officer, he had gone through such scenes many times before, for the number of people losing a son or daughter in such a way in any one given year is staggering.

After the officer had gone, with Ben and Sarah in the cruiser, for neither one could drive in their present condition, Dawn and Amy just sat in the living room, looking at each other, neither one being able to utter a word. Finally, Dawn as the oldest got up to walk over to where Amy was sitting, intending to put an arm around her. She knew that Amy, in losing her identical twin, was likely experiencing the loss of part of her own person. But as soon as Dawn started to walk across the living room, she felt a tremendous pain in her abdomen. Her knees buckled under her and she crumpled to the living room carpet. Dawn yelled at Amy to call an ambulance quick, as she was sure that something had gone wrong with the baby. The ambulance came in what seemed to Dawn like an eternity, but in actual fact was only twenty minutes. Dawn was quickly rushed to the hospital, and within an hour of arriving had given birth to a six and half pound little girl; Faith, the name she had chosen for her months ago. The reason

Dawn chose this name was not because she was turning religious, but because she had decided to have this child, believing that all would turn out for her in the end, even though her beginning in this life was in a less than ideal way, since she was not married and did not have a husband.

Amy had gone in the ambulance with Dawn and had not called her parents, not wanting to trouble them further at this time. She had just left a note with the maid, to give to her parents the moment they returned home. So when Ben and Sarah arrived home later that evening, with the police officer dropping them off at the door, they surely did not need any further news about ambulances and hospitals. Nevertheless, when duty calls, even in the midst of very trying circumstances, one needs to pull oneself up by the bootstrap and do what one needs to do, especially if one does not know God and is not in the habit of drawing upon Him for support, comfort, and direction. So Ben quickly reached for his cell phone and called his office manager, whom he knew was still in the office, as he had seen the lights on when they had gone by in the cruiser. He was an employee, but had also become a good family friend over the years. He was more than happy to now drive Ben and Sarah to the hospital, to see what had happened to Dawn. Neither of them wanted to think, since they were afraid that the reality might be that Dawn lost the baby, through the traumatic shock of hearing about the death of her younger sister.

But apprehension and unbearable grief momentarily at least turned to uplifted hearts as Ben and Sarah saw Dawn holding little Faith in her arms in that hospital bed. The irony of the moment had not yet sunk into their consciousness in that they had been given a granddaughter the very same day that they lost a daughter! The gift was certainly welcome, but the timing could not have been worse. Nevertheless, tears of joy fought with tears of grief as Ben and Sarah took turns holding little Faith in their arms. Little did they know that the tragic and sudden death of their beloved Zoe was to have a momentous effect on their family life for a few years to come, and in such unpredictable ways.

"For God so loved the world, that He gave His only begotten Son..."

John 3:16 in part

"But God demonstrates His own love toward us, in that while we were yet sinners, Christ died for us."

Romans 5:8

Chapter Six

/ Clouds, but with a silver lining

It has been well-said that the loss of a child is the worse suffering that parents can experience in this life. Many homes have been torn apart due to the grief experienced, often leaving behind a trail of broken lives, which sometimes are not mended before death comes calling. And so the momentary burst of joy at the birth of little Faith was soon replaced with the pain which comes and cannot be avoided when Ben and Sarah said their final goodbyes to Zoe, when she was buried three days later. The eulogy given by Amy, and the brief words spoken by her many friends, had kept everyone in tears all morning at the church service. And now at the graveside, Ben and Sarah are supporting each other, both fairly heavily sedated. Even after twenty years of marriage, they are still in love, so that what one was suffering, the other was also feeling. Therefore, one part of their pain was in losing Zoe, but another part was also in seeing one's loved one suffering. Even though neither of them had ever read the Bible, they were nevertheless experiencing what God says should happen to a husband and wife after marriage, which was that they were becoming as one. They wanted to offer support to the other, but neither one could due to the deep pain that each was experiencing.

In the months which followed, Dawn still lived at the house with little Faith, but soon found herself hiring a nanny, because her presence in her father's office was required more and more. Ben, who had been a non-drinker before, now started drinking on a regular basis. If it had been as a social drinker, it would not have been too bad, but it soon became a way for him to try to numb his pain. What he was not realizing is that he was trying to fix a situation with something which was not a solution. In other words, he needed to go through the grieving process, one step at a time, without looking for band-aid solutions. What he should have done every time he thought of Zoe was to allow whatever feelings he was experiencing to play themselves out. If he felt like crying, then he should just cry and not hold it back. If he was angry and blamed God for taking his daughter, then he should just let God know that, in whatever way he felt like expressing it, even if it meant yelling at God. In trying to drown his grief in alcohol, Ben was only suppressing his grief further and further from his consciousness. After a while, he was not feeling the pain of his loss, but then he was not feeling anything for anything or anyone else either. As a result, he found himself withdrawing within himself, not having much desire to interact with other members of his family, and not even wanting to have anything to do with managing the business of the resort.

And that is why much of the responsibility fell more and more on Dawn's shoulders as Ben withdrew further within himself each day. It was a good thing that Dawn was there, who although she only had a high school education, nevertheless found she having the natural abilities which were required for the tasks she was now facing. To be fair to Ben, he had been a good teacher, for he had taught her much of what he knew to do in the six months that Dawn worked in the office with him before the birth of little Faith. When one has a willing learner, then the learning curve becomes easier to maneuver through.

Under different circumstances, Ben's father, Jim, would have stepped in at this point and helped his son, especially since he still owned forty-nine percent of the resort, having given Ben and Sarah the controlling portion at the time of their marriage, which also made them instant multi-millionaires. However, Jim had two irons in the fire at the moment, which rendered him unavailable. He was in the midst of a run for the Senate in the upcoming midterm elections, as one of two Senators representing his state in Congress. And he was also in the planning stages for a casino to be next to the golf course at the resort. A friend of his owns about 260 acres there now, which is a cattle ranch, but he is getting old, has no sons, and wants to sell. Therefore, these two projects leave Jim, temporarily at least, unavailable to help at the resort.

In any case, the setup there is such that not much direct hands-on is required by Dawn, since there is an office manager in the offices at the road leading from the Interstate, where the restaurant, store, and clinic are, as part of one complex. He looks after all the bookings for the units by the lake and also after for the RV Park. In that office there is also an assistant, a secretary, a bookkeeper and a property maintenance manager. The golf course has its own manager of operations, since the club house is also a multilevel complex with its own bar, restaurant and meeting rooms, which can be rented out. All employees report to one of these three managers, who in turn report to Dawn, through a meeting in her office every Monday morning. Sometimes Ben is there, and sometimes he is not, having cultivated a set of drinking buddies that he hangs out with now. What has happened to her father weighs heavy on Dawn's heart, since they were so close before Zoe's untimely death.

If Ben had been alone in his inability to cope with the death of Zoe, then matters would not have been as bad for Dawn's family. However, Sarah, as the one who had to carry Zoe for nine months, it was as if one of her body parts had been torn away from her. At the time of the funeral, she had been placed on sleeping pills and sedatives by the family doctor, and now Sarah had become addicted to them. Whereas Ben used alcohol to try to numb his pain, Sarah used prescription drugs. She also was becoming numb to her feelings toward her family, and life in general. Whereas she should have been happy at being a grandmother to little Faith, who was always in the house with her, nevertheless, she just did not have it in her to go that needed step beyond herself.

The real surprise for Dawn was Amy. Whereas both her and Zoe had largely not been part of her life before, now Dawn noticed a change occurring. Although Amy did miss her sister, who was also her best friend, it seems she was able to go through the grieving process better than her parents. As a result, within six months of Zoe's passing, Amy started paying more and more attention to little Faith, playing with her whenever she could. Before long there was a bond forming between the two of them, which soon extended to Dawn, as Faith's mother. None of this is too difficult to understand here. With the parents being sidelined with grief which has for the moment made them unavailable to Dawn and Amy, it was inevitable in such a situation that the two sisters would draw closer to each other, finding there the comfort and love that their parents, for the time being at least, could not supply. As Dawn pondered this one day, she thought to herself that sometimes there is a silver lining to the dark clouds.

And so, as Dawn entered her twenties, all her energies were split between the love of her personal life, which was her daughter Faith, and the love of business, which was for the most part to give directions to Twin Peaks Resort, Golf, and RV Park. Her father was still there in the office some days, but his presence was never sure, due to sometimes being sober and sometimes not. Employees had come to respect Dawn, because they knew that the decisions she had made so far had been good ones. And who was to complain who had employment they enjoyed and workable management. It seemed by all appearances that Dawn's dream of one day marrying was now receding further and further to the back of her mind as each day progressed. However, as life would sometimes have it, it is when we are not looking for it, or expecting it, that love suddenly comes calling.

"There is an appointed time for everything. And there is a time for every event under heaven — A time to love..."

Eccles. 3:1,8 in part

Chapter Seven

/ Tom

Dawn got a call from the office manager one Sunday evening, letting her know that he would not be able to make their staff meeting in her office the next morning, because he had been sick all weekend, and was planning to make a trip into the city to see his doctor that Monday morning. Another reason for his call, was to ask her if she could fill in for him in interviewing a man who had called earlier the previous week wanting to rent a one bedroom unit on a year round basis. The office manager's assistant would normally handle such a duty, but as things had turned out, he was away on holidays at the moment. Since Dawn had never handled that part of the business before, she was more than happy to do so. She thought to herself that she did not often have direct contact with their guests, and that it would be nice for a change.

To Dawn that 2 pm appointment in the office manager's own office was to her just a routine business transaction. Interview the person, sign a lease for a year, take his money, and wish him a pleasant stay. However, when Tom was led to that office by the office secretary, Dawn's heart skipped a beat. It was not that Tom was tall, as he only appeared to be about five foot eight, which for Dawn, who was five foot six, was short. What took Dawn's breath away was that Tom was handsome, with beautiful green eyes and dark hair, and with a friendly smile. She rose to shake his hand, and found herself unable to speak. She just stood there holding his hand, for what seemed like a long time, but which was only about twenty seconds. Tom noticed her reaction to him, and it pleased him greatly, for what he saw in Dawn also pleased him. After all, we must remember that

Dawn, who was blond with sky blue eyes, still had not lost her figure, being only in her early twenties.

As Dawn finally collected her composure, she interviewed Tom, to ensure that he had a good character to be a resident at the resort on a yearly lease, finding out in the process that he was a Project Engineer, working for a consulting firm in the city. Since Tom had been born and raised in a small town in the Bible belt of the Midwest, he did not want to live in the city. When he found out that the resort rented out units on a year round basis, he thought he would look into it. And he had already gone back and forth on the Interstate and found out that he could get to work in twenty minutes, which is something he thought he could live with each day. After twenty-five minutes of talking with Tom, Dawn knew within herself that he would not be any trouble, and would in fact likely be an asset to the resort.

As they parted that afternoon, after signing a lease and exchanging a set of keys for money, both Tom and Dawn were thinking to themselves that they hoped to see each other again, although neither one revealed that to the other. Dawn was definitely attracted to Tom, but there was something about him that she could not put her finger on. He was very soft-spoken and seemed to have a tremendous sense of peace about him that she could not explain. He seemed to her like the kind of man who would not even hurt a house fly. For Tom's part, he was obviously attracted to Dawn by her external appearance, as he was after all a red-blooded male of the specie. But there was more to her. In being a mother and now a businesswoman, she exuded a level of self-confidence and maturity that was well beyond her youthful looks. And although Tom was now twenty-four, almost twenty-five, he had never met such a woman as this before.

And as a week went by, and then two, neither one had crossed paths again, but both Tom and Dawn still had each other very much in mind. So, it should not come as a surprise to anyone that they did see each other again. Some who do not know God would call it fate or a coincidence, but in reality it was neither, for to God there is neither fate nor coincidence, as all is being outworked from Heaven, to serve God's eternal purpose and glory. In fact, neither Tom nor Dawn planned this, at least at first. It was a Sunday, like many such days in this part of the country, where you want to be outside and

48

enjoy the sunshine and a view of the mountains nearby. Dawn had one of her friends from high school come over that afternoon, one of the few with whom she was still in contact. It seems that once Dawn had a child and business responsibilities, her priorities were no longer the same as those of her friends, who were focused on meeting men, settling down and raising a family. This is something, by the way, which is going the way of so many things which for millennia have given stability to society, namely, the nuclear family of husband, wife, and children.

In any case, this particular Sunday, Dawn and her friend Jill just sat by the pool at the house and chatted all afternoon. Then because Dawn did not want her to leave, she invited Jill to stay for the evening meal, which would take place by the pool, since it was too nice outside to go indoors. Faith was there, of course, and she was turning heads as her own mother had done before her, and still did, actually. Amy was now home for the summer, having just finished her first year of college away from home. She is still undecided as to what she wants to major in, but she knows for sure that she wants to work with children in some capacity, this having come about due to her own relationship with Faith, which she often wishes was her own child. Ben and Sarah are also there for a rare family meal together, with Sarah even having prepared the meal herself, instead of getting one of the hired staff to do it. Relations between them all is definitely not what they were before Zoe passed away, but one has to enjoy a gift from above when presented, as it was this day, for one never knows when there might be another.

After the meal, Jill suggests to Dawn that they take a walk down to the public beach area of the lake, something that Dawn has not done since she was in her teens, never having had occasion to do so since then. But now, to please her friend, she agrees. As they walk toward the lake together, Dawn shares with Jill for the first time her first meeting with Tom about two weeks ago. Jill's ears perk up when she hears Dawn talk about a man, and especially the way that she is relating it. It is obvious to Jill in the way that Dawn is saying this that she likes the guy. So when Dawn finishes speaking, Jill says that she hopes that they come across this Tom at the beach, for she would like to see him for herself. Dawn does not tell her friend this, but she is secretly hoping within herself to see Tom also.

When they reach the water's edge at the public beach area, Dawn looks toward the unit that Tom is renting, since she knows it is the second unit in from the pubic beach area. But she does not see Tom anywhere, neither in the water in front of the unit, nor on the veranda surrounding the front portion of the unit. So both Dawn and Jill stand there for a few more minutes looking in the other direction at all the people on the public beach. What neither of them is aware of, is that Tom, who had earlier been sitting on the veranda, had gone in to the washroom for a moment and to get himself another lemonade. After sitting down outside again, he could not help noticing these two women standing there by the water's edge by themselves, only about 300 feet away. When his gaze had focused even better, he was sure that the blond standing there was Dawn, who had interviewed him. Then his wondering turned to absolute certainty, so that when both women looked in his direction again as they appeared to be leaving, Tom instinctively lifted an arm and waved to them. Dawn knew without a doubt that this was Tom. And she also instinctively started to walk toward Tom's unit, with Jill scurrying to keep up with her, knowing that she was now going to meet this Tom fella. When they came within a few yards of where Tom was, Tom called out 'hello' to Dawn and Jill, inviting them to come and enjoy a lemonade with him on the veranda.

So after exchanging greetings and an introduction, and while Jill sat on one of the outside padded chairs, Dawn followed Tom back into the unit, as he went in to get the lemonade. Tom let her know, now that they were in private, that he was glad to see her again. And of course Dawn did not want to hold back from Tom her own excitement at seeing him again, although Tom could already see it written all over her face, and in her body language. Oftentimes we communicate more with our bodies than we do with words, and this is what was here happening between Tom and Dawn.

As Tom poured the drinks, Dawn glanced into the living room, which was just beside the kitchen area, wanting to see if this guy was a messy guy or not, and what caught her eye was a wooden clock on a far wall, which had 'Jesus is Lord,' written across it. Not being very religious herself, in fact not having been in a church building for the last few years, especially since Zoe's tragic fatal accident, Dawn was now struck by seeing this clock. What did this mean, she wondered? But before she could come to some sort of conclusion in her mind,

Tom was beside her with the two drinks, and noticed her gazing at the clock. So without saying a word, he walked into the living room, motioning for Dawn to come also. What he wanted her to see was the other plaques that he had on his wall, with one saying "Trust in The Lord with all your heart, acknowledge Him, and He will direct your paths," and another saying, "With God all things are possible." When Tom knew that Dawn had finished reading these, he told her that he had a few more in his bedroom and even one in the washroom. But before they could get into a conversation as to what this all meant, they both realized at the same time that Jill was sitting outside by herself and must be wondering what happened to the two of them. So without either of them saying a word, they walked out the door to the veranda.

""Do not be bound together with unbelievers…"

2 Cor. 6:14 in part

Chapter Eight

/ A baring of souls

Before Dawn and Jill had left Tom's unit that memorable Sunday evening, he had asked her out for a coffee the following Monday evening. Dawn had said she had a prior engagement that night, but would be free the Tuesday evening. Now it was 6:50 pm at the house, and Dawn is looking out the living room window, same as her mother had done when Dave had brought her home that evening, which now seemed like a long time ago. Tom was not coming in, just picking her up at the door, which had been as per Dawn's instructions, when she gave him directions on how to get to her place. For up to now, Tom did not know that Dawn was the daughter of the man who owned the resort, that they were wealthy, that she had a daughter, and what had happened to her family since the death of Zoe. She has intentions of telling him sometime, not knowing when would be the best occasion.

So when Dawn finally did spot Tom driving in through the main gates of their property, she made her way to the front door and out, and was standing outside when Tom's car pulled up beside her. After exchanging greetings, Tom pulled away, and as he did, Dawn mentioned that she did not want to have a coffee here at the resort, but preferred to go into the city. Actually, Tom was happy to hear this, since he had been at both the restaurant at the property and the one at the golf course clubhouse, and also preferred to go into the city for coffee. As they drove, they chatted away as if they had known each other all their lives, both being very glad to be in each other's company. When they reached the city, Tom suggested to Dawn that they pick up coffees to go and then he would drive by his place of work and where he used to live before. After they had done so, and while they were sitting in the car in front of the apartment complex where he used to live, Tom thought he would also show Dawn where he attended church. And without saying a word, he proceeded to drive there. By this point, Dawn was fully trusting Tom, and did not even question where he was taking her. So when he reached the church buildings, he just parked out front and shut off the engine. Dawn took one look at the church, read the sign, which also had a Bible verse underneath, "Jesus said, "I am the way the truth and the life,"" and then she turned to look at Tom. This brought back to her mind the verses, which she had assumed were from the Bible, which she had read on Tom's walls at the unit a couple of nights ago. Tom was glad when Dawn asked him about the verses, because one of the things that Tom wanted to do before he went any further in his relationship with Dawn was to tell her about his faith in God.

But Tom did not want to sit in front of the church buildings all night, so he suggested to Dawn that they drive up to a spot he knew, which was a park overlooking the river below and the mountains in the distance towards the west. There they could sit and talk, while they watched the sun go down. It was a spot that Dawn was already very familiar with, having grown up in the area, and having gone to school in the city, plus having come here to park with some of her boyfriends in the past. But now it was entirely different. Now it was with a man for whom she had a different set of feelings, shall we say, more mature feelings. In any case, Dawn too now planned to tell Tom all about Faith, the business, and her family problems, before they returned home that evening. It was now 8:30 pm, still lots of time to talk.

But Tom first, since she had already asked him a question back at the church buildings. So what Tom related to her in brief that evening was almost totally foreign to her. He told her that he was a Christian, with Dawn being glad to hear, since she also regarded herself as a Christian. But when Tom said that he had a personal relationship with God, then Dawn knew that this was something totally different. So Tom explained that he was not a Christian in name only, but that at the age of fourteen, which was ten years ago, he had heard a message at special services at the church his family attended back home, where the preacher had said that one needed to be born again in order to enter the Kingdom of God. Since that kind of language was strange to Tom, he perked up to hear the explanation, and when the preacher concluded his message that evening, he bent his head in the pew and asked God to meet his need of knowing Him as he knew his parents did. He had been under deep conviction of sins before coming to this special service that his church was hosting, and now in having heard that God's Son, Jesus Christ, had died for his sins on that cross over two thousand years ago, then after being buried, had been raised from the dead so as to be alive forevermore to grant him eternal life with God. So Tom had felt his need of God's forgiveness of his sins that night and had called upon God to forgive him, based on the death of God's own Son having died in His place the death that was due him. And as he did so, he suddenly felt like a huge load of sins had been removed from his shoulders and a peace filled his heart that he had never known before, only finding out afterwards that God had just come to indwell him by His Holy Spirit, making him there and then a child of God forever and ever.

As Tom spoke, Dawn listened, realizing within herself that this was something that was totally foreign to her experience and had never heard such things until now. She liked what she saw in Tom, so she could not criticize any of what she heard, although she did not understand most of it. Many questions were coming to her mind, but she decided that they would have to wait for another day. She had things to say to Tom, and she noticed on her watch that it was now nine-thirty, with the sun making its descent just behind the mountains on the horizon. So Dawn looked at Tom again and said that she too had something to share with him. Then she proceeded to tell him about Faith, first of all, for that was the good part, only being sorry that her birth had taken place out of wedlock and without a father for her to know. She mentioned Dave and the fact that she had not seen him since the night they broke off. Then she related that Faith's birth had taken place the very night that her younger sister had died in a car accident. Now it was Tom's turn to just sit and listen in part wonder and part sadness, as Dawn went on to relate the effect this death had on her parents, which was continuing even to this day, which was now a little over two years later. She also related to Tom her involvement in the resort since that time. All these things left Tom speechless, as he just sat there and pondered all the things which Dawn had just shared with him.

Since Dawn had said when he picked her up that she would like to be back home by eleven, since her day started early, one reason being that she liked to spend an hour with Faith each morning before she went to the office. She normally took her lunch break with Faith again, and then was usually off around 4:30 pm. Dawn was glad that Amy was home for the summer, for that meant she knew Faith was with someone who loved her deeply, instead of just being with a nanny, who was a relative stranger, as it had proven difficult to find one who stayed for any length of time. In any case, when Tom's car pulled up in front of Dawn's home, he took her left hand in his right hand and told her that he had really enjoyed their evening together. Dawn said that she had also and invited Tom in for an evening meal to meet Faith and the rest of the family the next evening. But Tom said he could not, as he had a prayer meeting at the church that evening, which he was not in the habit of missing. So Dawn invited him for the Thursday night, which Tom accepted without reservations, as he especially wanted to meet Faith.

"and said to Him, "Do You hear what these children are saying?" And Jesus said to them, "Yes; have you never read, 'Out of the mouth of infants and nursing babies You have prepared praise for Yourself'?"

Matthew 21:16

Chapter Nine

/ Tom meets the family

As Dawn woke up Thursday morning, she had only one thought on her mind, which was Tom, and wondering how things would work out when Tom came for supper that evening. What Dawn did not know was that Tom was at this very moment on his knees, having his morning devotions, before he showered and shaved, and headed into the city for work, picking up his breakfast and lunch at the restaurant on the property as he went by. One of the things Tom had mentioned to his church family the evening before, when at the prayer meeting, was that he had met this young woman who was not a Christian, but that in his heart had felt that she might be the woman God had for him. He had said that he did not want the relationship to get deeper without Dawn coming to know God, so he had asked his church family, who were there, to please pray for him and especially Dawn.

At about 11 am, Dawn heard car doors opening and shutting outside, and so got up from her desk in the office and peered out the window. There were two limousines which had just pulled up, and she noticed that out of one emerged her grandfather, Jim, and his wife Dot, plus two men, then from the other limo about six other men, whom she did not know. Dawn wondered to herself what this all meant, as she had not heard mention of her father's parents coming this day, let alone with guests. Ben was away at the moment, no one knowing where he was, but Sarah was home, as was Amy and Faith. When Dawn reached the front door, her mother Sarah was already greeting her husband's parents and being introduced to the guests.

As it turned out, Jim had flown in on his private plane to the city, where he had arranged for two limos to meet the group, having brought with him the men who would be partnering with him in the proposed casino. Jim had lost the Senate race that he had entered, and as a result had been devoting all his time in making the casino a reality. This would be the consortium's first look at the proposed site, before having invited dignitaries and the press there at 4 pm for a news conference, to publicly announce the project. Jim had already contacted the golf club restaurant and had made arrangements for the group and guests to have an evening meal there. Now they were all at the house to meet Jim's family and especially to have the whole family at the site at 4 pm also. What Dawn also found out is that her father knew about this already, but somehow had neglected to tell her. Obviously the alcohol was also affecting Ben's memory, Dawn thought to herself.

When Dot had heard that Jim was planning to go to the resort, which meant an opportunity to visit with her granddaughters, and especially little Faith, she had insisted to her husband that he take her along. Now as Jim spent the afternoon with the group, visiting the resort, the unit area, the RV area, and the site, plus having a private meeting, Dot used this time to visit with Sarah, Dawn, Amy, and Faith at the house. It was then that she heard about this Tom, whom Dawn had recently met, and who was coming over for supper at 6 pm that evening to meet the family. And now that the whole family was expected at the site, plus at the meal at the golf club afterwards, Dawn was now in a real quandary as to what she should do. Should she call Tom and have him come some other evening, she thought to herself. But to her delight, her grandmother's reaction of hearing that her granddaughter was seeing a man was the same as what her friend Jill's had been, in terms of her also wanting to meet him. And since Dot mentioned that the whole group was scheduled to fly back home later that evening, then meeting Tom would somehow have to take place that evening.

It was now 2:30 pm and the family was getting ready to be at the site of the proposed casino for 4 pm. Dawn had already discussed it with her mother and grandmother, and it had been decided that Tom would also be invited for the evening meal at least, so that Dawn's grandparents could also meet him, before they left for home. This was not what Dawn had envisioned, but sometimes you have to do with what life throws at you. Sometimes, events have a way of being unpredictable, somewhat like the weather, as anyone knows who lives near mountains. In now knowing at which consulting firm Tom worked at, she looked it up in the phone book and calls there, asking to speak to Tom. Thankfully he is available to take a call, and Dawn quickly explains the sudden change of plans, due to the arrival of her grandparents and the group at the resort. Finally Dawn asks Tom if there is any possibility of him being at her house for 3:30 pm. For a few moments, there is silence at Tom's end, as he is thinking within himself about this situation and what he should do. Then he says to Dawn to stay on the line as he goes and talks with his boss. And before Dawn can respond, Tom had put down the receiver and is on way to his manager's office. Within two or three minutes, Tom is back saying that his boss said that he could leave that moment, with his boss knowing that Tom was a good employee, who deserved such consideration once in a while.

When Tom arrives at the house at 3:30 pm, the two limos are there, as the whole group has gathered at the house now and are planning to go to the proposed casino site from there at 3:45 pm. No one has had time to yet tell Jim that Tom has also been invited. As the doorbell rings, for no one had heard Tom drive up with all the commotion, everyone came to a standstill, with everyone stopping to speak at once. It was kind of eerie the way that happened, but Dawn suddenly realized that this must be Tom, so she proceeds to answer the door, with little Faith in tow, whom she had just put down in order to go to the door. Dawn is so happy to see Tom that she gives him a big hug after inviting him in. When little Faith sees her mother hugging Tom, she suddenly exclaims, to everyone's utter amazement, "Daddy." After the initial shock, all in Dawn's immediate family, apart from her grandparents, immediately erupt into laughter, which brings a big smile on Faith's face and an even bigger grin on Tom's.

The project announcement went off without a hitch at 4 pm and following, with the city mayor and many of the city administration also being there, plus about thirty members of the press, including four of the TV stations from the city, which had sent crews to cover the event live. This was to be the state's first big casino, so there was a lot of interest from many parties, some even being negative, as there were also protesters there. Actually, the casino was likely one reason

Jim had lost the Senate run, as his opponent had heard of it and had made it an issue in the campaign, being fervently against gambling. Obviously many people were against it also. But no one would have guessed that to be the case that afternoon, for apart from a handful of protesters, everyone there seemed to be beaming with delight that this project was going forward.

This was not the way Dawn had envisioned Tom meeting her family, but then there are events in life that one cannot plan for, but in the end are for the best, even though at the time, one could not have predicted that. This was one of them. For what happened that evening, before Jim and Dot left for the city and then home with the group they had come with, is that Tom got to talk with Jim, Ben, and Dawn privately, where the two men found out that Tom was a Project Engineer, with a well-known consulting firm in the city, which was one of the firms that had bid for part of the work on the casino. What none of them could predict at this point was the extent Tom would eventually be involved in all the lives of this family, but not in ways that anyone could have ever predicted at that point in time.

God works in mysterious ways His wonders to perform!

Chapter Ten

/ More of the unexpected

Before the private meeting had ended that Thursday evening, Dawn had invited Tom over for supper on the Saturday evening at the house, with her father having heartily consented. Dawn had thought that it was not fair to Tom, nor to the family, to have met under such rush circumstances. She too had felt in her heart that this might be the man for her, chuckling to herself every time she remembered what her daughter Faith had exclaimed upon seeing Tom. Yes, indeed, what does come out of the mouths of babes and infants! It is now almost 6 pm on the Saturday, and Tom is eagerly anticipated by all. Even Sarah and Amy had really liked Tom. Not only was Amy growing envious of her older sister's daughter, now she was also growing envious of the man she had met. But the news that Tom would be bringing Dawn was not likely to please her. Thankfully Tom had decided to wait until after the meal before telling Dawn what had happened to him.

The meeting of clans and the meal was not as hectic as it had been on the Thursday evening. It was much more relaxed and enjoyable in the family's formal dining room. There had been no further surprising exclamations from Faith, but Ben had surprised the whole family when he had asked Tom to say 'grace' before the meal. This was not a usual family practice, but Ben had thought of it after Dawn had told him about Ben's deep religious faith. Now with the meal over and everyone having retired to the comfort of the living room, Tom slowly begins to tell Dawn and her family that he is being sent to South America. He had only found out about this himself when he had returned to work the Friday morning. One of the firm's project managers, who was overseeing a hydroelectric project that the firm had designed, had fallen ill, possibly from malaria, although it had not yet been determined with certainly. Since Tom had worked extensively on that project, and he was now the only one available to send, he was being asked to go as a replacement until the current manager could get back to work again. Tom had been told that this could take from a few weeks to a few months. Although Tom did not want to be away from Dawn, yet at the same time he did not want to let the firm down in their time of time, for his decision here would more than likely have a great impact upon his future. And so, he had told his boss he would go. And now he is to fly out this coming Sunday afternoon.

While Dawn's heart sank upon hearing what she just heard, she was now growing as a businesswoman in her own right, and could readily understand the situation, although on a personal level, it was not an easy one to easily accept. Her heart had grown even heavier when she drove Tom to the airport in the city on the Sunday afternoon, accompanied by Amy and Faith, who had come along for the ride. Tom had held Dawn a long time, before doing the same with Amy and Faith. One thing Tom knew for sure is that he had fallen in love with Dawn, and also Faith, whom he regarded as just a miniature version of her mother. This parting, which no one had seen coming just two days prior, was to turn out for the best in the long run. As the English poet and hymn writer, William Cowper, had once written, 'God does indeed work in mysterious ways His wonders to perform.' Tom already knew for sure that there is a God in Heaven, but now he was to find out just how much God was able to work even though Tom was not there.

"also we have obtained an inheritance, having been predestined according to His purpose who works all things after the counsel of His will…"

Ephesians 1:11

Chapter Eleven

/ A sleepless night and a longing for Tom

Dawn leans over and looks at the alarm clock beside her bed. It says 3 am and Dawn's feelings sink even lower. Three more hours and it will be time to get up to spend time with Faith before her day at the office starts. She has been unable to sleep all night, thinking about Tom, who has only been gone a mere twelve hours. Dawn cannot remember a sleepless night like this. Even the day Zoe died, she slept like a log that night, although it is true that she had gone through her final labor pains that day and had given birth to Faith. That certainly takes a lot out of a woman, something that a man could never truly know. As Dawn lies on her back and tries to sleep, her thoughts keep going back to Tom, playing a game of 'what if' in her mind. What if Tom gets malaria and dies down there? What if the manager dies and Tom is asked to take over the position permanently until the project is completed? That could mean Tom being away from her for a very long time. Finally, she has to end this game and tries to think of something else.

One thought which comes to her mind is just how much she had enjoyed Tom's prayer before the meal the other night. It was just as if God were present with them in the room, she thought. But what Dawn did not realize as she thinks this is that she was the only one in her family who sensed this. In other words, God is now at work in her life, drawing her to Himself. He is in the process of bringing Tom and Dawn together in a lifelong relationship, but before that can happen, He needs to bring Dawn into a personal relationship with Himself. And so in the Sovereignty of God, He arranges for Tom to be away for a while, while He works Providentially – that is, working His wonders behind the scene of the seen. Another thought which Dawn has here is just how much her family likes Tom. Even her father and mother appear to have a totally new outlook these days. Are they, as parents, somehow sensing that they are about to gain a son-in-law? It must be remembered here that in many cultures around the world, it is the parents who chooses the spouse for their children to marry. And when done with their son or daughter's wellbeing in mind, and not their own, then those marriages more often than not are good choices. In other words, parents have a knack for knowing the right person for their son or daughter. Foolish is the son or daughter who thinks he or she knows better than their parents and marries someone the parents do not agree with. Many such marriages have failed due to the stubbornness of the son or daughter wanting to do one's own will.

Just as Dawn starts to doze off, the alarm suddenly goes off, and Dawn thinks to herself just how cruel life can be at times, this being one of them. But her thoughts of self-pity evaporate an hour later, after she has washed and dressed, and is now sitting in the kitchen with Faith, enjoying breakfast together before they spend some quality time in the living room and outside for a little stroll before Dawn goes to the office in the house for 8:30 pm. The three managers will be in at 9 am for their weekly staff meeting, which usually lasts until lunchtime, with the group generally having lunch in the resort restaurant afterwards.

As Dawn and Faith start to leave for a little stroll, Amy comes downstairs and meets them at the door, wanting to go along. When they walk outside, they notice that their parents are already out by the pool, having eaten their breakfast out there this morning, without anyone else being aware of it. Now Dawn and the others make their way over to them. After hugs are given to little Faith, Ben tells Dawn and Amy that he and Sarah have decided that it is time that they take a holiday together, something they have not done since Zoe died over two years ago. They thought they would fly to Paris, in France, then rent a car and drive through various countries in Europe, such as Germany, Switzerland, and Italy. They are not sure how long that will take, but they will call in once in a while to find out how things are going at home, and will give them an update at that time. Ben says they will be flying out this Wednesday, asking Dawn to drive them to the airport in the family Lincoln, which will allow enough room for Amy and Faith to also go along.

Amy is getting ready to resume her studies at College in a couple of weeks, and now with her parents planning to be away, Dawn suddenly misses Tom even more, but at the same time really glad to have Faith to occupy her thoughts and to channel her love to. How important to have an outlet for love, Dawn realizes within herself as she lies on her bed this Monday evening. Another thought which occurs to Dawn is that while they are in the city on Wednesday, she should drop in at a bookstore and pick up a map and a book about Brazil, for that is where Tom is. He has promised to call her each Sunday evening, and when he calls, she can ask him the name of the place he is at, which she can then locate on the map. Then she remembers Jill and wonders if she might not be able to meet them at the Westside mall, knowing that she lives in that area. Then possibly they could all have lunch together before returning to the resort. This is one thing Dawn likes about the life situation she has been born into, she has the financial resources needed to meet any of her wants and she can also take time off anytime she wants to. Feeling somewhat satisfied with these thoughts, she now dozes off to a much better sleep before she realizes it.

"So faith comes from hearing, and hearing by the word of Christ."

Romans 10:17

Chapter Twelve

/ Dawn discovers a whole new world

It is 8 am on Wednesday, Ben is driving to the airport in his Lincoln, with Sarah beside him, and Dawn, Faith, and Amy in the backseat. Their flight leaves at 9:30 am, but they are required to be at the airport an hour before flight time, to check in and to then go through security. Jill has agreed to meet Dawn and the others in the food court at the Westside Mall for 10 am for coffee. Dawn and Jill have not seen each other since Jill was over at the house a few weeks ago. It will be nice to see her again. Good friends are hard to come by, and when we find one, we need to do all we can to keep them, Dawn thinks to herself as they drive to the mall after having hugged and kissed their parents goodbye.

After coffee, they stroll down to a bookstore Dawn knows about located in the mall. And when they get there, she is really glad that they have a few travel books of Brazil, and although there is no single map of the country, there is one inside a set of maps on all countries of South America, which she purchases. Then as she makes her way to the cash register, she notices a section of the store on religious books and Bibles. She suddenly remembers that the Tuesday night Tom shared his faith at the park, overlooking the river and the city, he had encouraged Dawn to read the life story of Jesus, in the four accounts given by Matthew, Mark, Luke, and John, in the New Testament portion of the Bible. Tom had just assumed that Dawn had a Bible at home, but in fact she did not, having been afraid to divulge that information to Tom at the time. So with Jill by her side, while Amy is with Faith on a bench just outside the store, Dawn buys her first Bible ever. Then as she is about to walk away with the Bible she has chosen for herself, she notices some Bibles for toddlers, and there and then decides to also purchase one for her daughter. What is good for the gander is also good for the goose, she thinks to herself, or is that the other way around? Whatever, she concludes.

Later that evening, as Dawn pulls out the Toddler's Bible, which she purchased for Faith, she does not realize that she is on a journey, with God very much at work, which will eventually have life-changing consequences, both for her and Faith, and for her whole family. And so it was not a coincidence that she picked up a Bible for herself and Faith earlier that morning. God is at work in her life now, working as unseen behind the scenes, although she is not aware of it yet. When Dawn reads a couple of stories of the life of Jesus, which have been tailored for toddlers, she suddenly wishes that she had been read such stories when she was Faith's age. Then in finishing the second story and noticing that Faith has fallen asleep, she hugs and kisses her and tucks her in, closing the light. And since this is way too early for Dawn to retire for the night, she makes her way downstairs, to one of the comfort chairs in the living room, with her own first Bible in hand.

Much of what Dawn reads is not understood, as she begins in Matthew's account, as suggested by Tom. And what really captures her attention is reading in the very first chapter that Jesus was actually born of a virgin. 'Wow,' Dawn exclaims to herself. How can this be? Oh, yes, she just read, "the Child Who has been born in her is of The Holy Spirit," not fully understanding what that meant either. 'Questions to ask Tom on Sunday,' Dawn thinks to herself. Then, with her interest having been aroused at this point, and because this has only taken about ten minutes to read, Dawn decides to continue reading. Then without realizing it, Amy comes down to the living room from her bedroom around 9:30 pm, and finds Dawn still reading. She asks Dawn what she is reading, and when told that it is the Bible she purchased earlier that day, she just exclaims, 'Oh,' and walks right back upstairs, finding it strange that her sister has now started to read the Bible. Then suddenly she remembers Tom, and then everything starts falling into place. And before Dawn retires that night, she finishes reading to the end of Matthew, the eleventh chapter. And there one verse near the end of that chapter arrests her attention, where she reads Jesus saying, "Come to Me, all who are weary and heavy-laden, and I will give you rest." 'Rest,' Dawn thinks to herself, would that ever be nice. Rest for her anxious soul. Rest from all her fears. Rest from her guilty feelings relating to her past. Rest about her future with Tom. But what does "Come to Me," mean? At this point, Dawn is confident that Tom will know the answer to her questions, and cannot wait for him to call Sunday night at 7 pm, as he said he would. To Dawn, that cannot come soon enough.

When 7 pm does arrive Sunday night, Dawn is sitting by the phone in the living room, having already put Faith to bed, this night having asked Amy to read her a couple of stories from the Toddler's Bible. And now she sits and waits. Then 7 pm is finally here, and then 7:10 pm, but no ringing of the phone. Then 7:20, and now Dawn is really starting to wonder what happened to Tom, with her mind starting its 'what ifs' again. Then at 7:28 pm the phone finally rings, and it is Tom. He apologizes, saying that he had been requested to a site meeting by the contractor that afternoon, to handle a problem that had come up that day. The project had a tight schedule, with work continuing on a seven day twenty-four hours a day basis.

It has only been a week, and they have only known each other for a few weeks, yet now Tom and Dawn talk as two people definitely in love, no doubt as Ben and Sarah would have talked to each other before they were married, and before Zoe died. Then after asking Tom where he is in Brazil and writing it down with the correct spelling, Dawn lets him know that she has purchased a set of maps of South America, which includes Brazil, and also a travel book of Brazil. Now she can look up where he is and where the hydroelectric project is taking place, even looking up the river it is on.

Then she springs the biggest surprise of all on Tom, which makes his heart skip a beat when he hears of it at the other end of the line. She lets him know first of all that earlier in the week her parents left for a holiday in Europe, and while in the city, she picked up a Bible at a bookstore. She has now finished reading the book of John, which is the fourth of the books Tom had earlier asked her to read of the accounts of Jesus' life while on earth. And now Dawn cannot wait to get to the questions she has for Tom, since there are certain things she cannot understand. Actually, without really realizing it, Dawn is now between two opinions, not knowing which one to believe. On the one hand, she wants to believe that Jesus really is The Son of God, as He claimed to be, and which all the miracles He did and the things

He said pointed to Him as being. And on the other hand, there was what the religious leaders of His day were saying, who claimed that Jesus was just a mere man, like any other man, and not The Son of God at all. Were they right?

With this being the place that Dawn is at spiritually, she now asks Tom her first question, which is why Jesus had to be born of a virgin? Why not a birth like any other human being? When Tom hears this, he now realizes that God is at work here and has just presented him with a golden opportunity to share the gospel with Dawn. So Tom explains that Jesus is not just a mere human being, but rather is The Son of God, Who is eternally existing, but Who in time, did come from Heaven to this earth to take on a human body like we have. At this point, Tom asks Dawn to turn over to the book of Hebrews, at the tenth chapter, and then guides her to find it, and then has her read aloud at verses five to seven, "Therefore, when He comes into the world, He says, "Sacrifice and offering You have not desired, but a body You have prepared for Me; in whole burnt offerings and sacrifices for sin You have taken no pleasure. Then I said, 'Behold, I have come (In the scroll of the book it is written of Me) to do Your will, O God.' " So Tom explains to Dawn, when she finishes reading this aloud, that God The Father prepared a body in the womb of a virgin girl named Mary, who was a believer, which body was for His eternally existing Son to take on, and then to be born of her as 'Jesus Christ.' And the reason it had to be of a virgin, continued Tom, is that God is Holy, that is, without sin, while we are sinful creatures since the time of Adam and Eve, when our first parents sinned against God.

Dawn interjected at this point and said to Tom that she had thought that Adam and Eve were just fictitious characters. Tom explained that they were the first couple created by God directly, from whom the whole human race derived its existence, all coming from this original pair. But one important point which must be realized at this point, continued Tom, is that when God created Adam and Eve, they were innocent, meaning that they were sinless, never having sinned and not even knowing what sin was. So in order to teach them what sin was, God gave them a command, which went like this, "The Lord God commanded the man, saying, "From any tree of the garden you may eat freely; but from the tree of the knowledge of good and evil you shall not eat, for in the day that you eat from it you will surely die." " Tom went on to explain that God then relates that a day did come when Adam and Eve did disobey God by partaking of the forbidden tree, thereby sinning against God the first sin ever committed by human beings. What this also meant, explained Tom, is that Adam and Eve were no longer innocent human beings, but now sinners in God's sight. They had not only personally sinned, but they had now incurred a sinful nature, in that all they would now do, say, and think, would be sinful in God's sight. And this would of course have a disastrous effect on the whole of the human race, continued Tom. 'How so,' asked Dawn.

At this point Tom had Dawn pick up her Bible again and this time guided her to find the book of Romans, then chapter five, reading aloud at verse 12, "Therefore, just as through one man sin entered into the world, and death through sin, and so death spread to all men, because all sinned..." So Tom continued, as Dawn finished reading, and said that sin entered the whole of the human race through Adam, in that the sinful nature that they now had was transmitted through the male to their offspring, with the process repeating itself all the way from their day to their own, with each person becoming personally accountable to God for one's own sins at the age of accountability, which is the age each of us reach when what is good and what is evil is consciously known, and then whenever we do freely choose the evil we become a sinner in God's sight, personally accountable to Him for the sin just committed. That is why, explained Tom, that our parents do not have to teach us how to sin, but rather to attempt to restrain us, simply because once we become sinners at the age of accountability, thereby incurring a sinful nature, we from then on sin naturally, because it is part of our nature. And that is also why, Tom continued, that God can say to the whole human race, "for all have sinned and fall short of the glory of God," now quoting this to Dawn from memory.

There was a long pause at Dawn's end here, as she was assimilating all this in her heart and mind, with Tom realizing this and not wanting to intervene in what he knew that God was likely doing at this point. Then when prompted by God to continue, Tom went on to explain to Dawn that this was why God's Son, when His time came for Him to take on the human body prepared by His Father on earth, it had to be through a virgin, so that His Son would not incur the sinful nature inherited from Adam, and passed on by the male of the human race.

Things were now falling into place for Dawn, as God was illuminating His word and Tom's explanation to her.

Then Tom continued and went on to say that after Jesus Christ had lived a perfect life, as sinless and in complete obedience to every command of His Father, thereby carrying out His will only, that He then died in the place of all human sinners of time, paying in His death the penalty due the sin of the whole human race. Tom read, from his own Bible this time, the verses which he had Dawn read earlier, namely that when Adam and Eve ate of the forbidden tree, they would die, because the penalty for disobedience, which was sin, was death. And then reading again at Romans chapter five and verse twelve, that death spread to the whole human race, because all sinned.

This was now all becoming crystal clear to Dawn. Without needing anyone to ask her whether she was a sinner before a holy God, she knew without a doubt that she was. She vividly remembered how she had rushed into sin willingly with Dave, time and again after having lost her virginity. So again, after a long pause, when Tom asked her if she would like to personally know God, Dawn answered 'Yes,' without hesitation. She remembered Jesus' statement that she had read earlier from Matthew the eleventh chapter, which she had not understood, where Jesus had said, "Come to Me, all who are weary and heavy-laden, and I will give you rest." Now God was letting her know in her spirit that knowing God personally, as Tom had just asked her of doing, what the same as what Jesus said here, "Come to Me."

So Tom, in being guided by God here, plus remembering what he had learned in the evangelism class he had sat in at the church he attended, simply then led Dawn to find and read aloud a few verses of God's word, beginning with Romans, the third chapter, at verse 23, which he had earlier quoted to her, "for all have sinned and fall short of the glory of God..." Tom asked Dawn at this point if what God said about all having sinned also included her, to which Dawn replied that it did. Then Tom had Dawn turn to Romans, the fifth chapter, this time reading at verse 8, "But God demonstrates His own love toward us, in that while we were yet sinners, Christ died for us." Now the question Tom had for Dawn was whether she was included in the statement from God that Christ, God's Son, had died for all sinners, when He died at the cross. Again, Dawn, without hesitation, replied, 'Yes.' Then Tom had Dawn turn two pages over to Romans chapter six and asked her to read verse twenty-three, where she read, "For the wages of sin is death, but the free gift of God is eternal life in Christ Jesus our Lord." This time Tom asked Dawn if she wanted from God His free gift of eternal life in His Son, Jesus Christ. Again, Dawn replied in the affirmative.

Then Tom continued and said to Dawn to turn to the book of Corinthians, which he again helped her find, and then at the fifteenth chapter reading there verses three and four aloud, "For I delivered to you as of first importance what I also received, that Christ died for our sins according to the Scriptures, and that He was buried, and that He was raised on the third day according to the Scriptures..." After Tom had paused for a few seconds to let these verses sink into Dawn's consciousness, no doubt being led by God here, he then said to Dawn that he had one last passage for her to read, directing her to the book of Romans again, and this time had her read aloud from the tenth chapter, at verse nine to thirteen, where she read, "that if you confess with your mouth Jesus as Lord, and believe in your heart that God raised Him from the dead, you will be saved; for with the heart a person believes, resulting in righteousness, and with the mouth he confesses, resulting in salvation. For the Scripture says, "Whoever believes in Him will not be disappointed." For there is no distinction between Jew and Greek; for the same Lord is Lord of all, abounding in riches for all who call on Him; for "Whoever will call on the name of the Lord will be saved."

At this point, Tom said to the woman he knew without a shadow of a doubt that he loved, and also now knew that God had led him to, 'Dawn, will you call on God at this time so as to come to know Him personally, doing so either aloud or silently to yourself?' Having never gone through what she was now going through, Dawn simply said to Tom that she preferred doing so silently. And so, where she was, she bent her head and closed her eyes, saying, 'Dear God, I need you to help me. I do believe that Your Son died for me when he died at the cross, and that You indeed did raise Him again from the dead.' At the very moment Dawn finished saying this, she was very much aware of the Presence of God in the room with her, just as she had sensed God's Presence when Dave had prayed at her house not that long ago. It was as if God was now extending a Hand to her, to take her across the threshold from unbelief to faith in Him. And as she saw herself grasp God's Hand in her heart and mind, she sensed such a peace and a joy flowing over her soul that she knew without a doubt that she was now a child of God and that she just had all her sins forgiven.

Tom was praying while he waited on the other end of the line, and was overcome with joy when he heard Dawn exclaim out loud to him, "Tom, God just touched me, and I have no doubt that I now know Him. Please do not ask me to explain, for I just know." Of course Tom had gone through the same experience, so he indeed knew what she meant. So at this point, he had Dawn take her Bible again, and this time guided her to find and then read aloud the First John, near the end of the Bible, at the fifth chapter, reading from verse nine to verse thirteen, where Dawn now read, "If we receive the testimony of men, the testimony of God is greater; for the testimony of God is this, that He has testified concerning His Son. The one who believes in the Son of God has the testimony in himself; the one who does not believe God has made Him a liar, because he has not believed in the testimony that God has given concerning His Son. And the testimony is this, that God has given us eternal life, and this life is in His Son. He who has the Son has the life; he who does not have the Son of God does not have the life. These things I have written to you who believe in the name of the Son of God, so that you may know that you have eternal life." You see, Dawn, said Tom, God wants you to have the assurance in your heart that you now have eternal life from Him as a free gift, simply from having believed in His Son, Jesus Christ, as you now have. At this point, Dawn could hardly contain herself, being so filled with love, for Dave, yes, but especially for God, for just having opened her heart to believe in Him, as she now did.

Tom now realized that it was quite late, so he advised Dawn to call someone when she could, someone who was close to her, and to tell that person what had just happened to her. Then he said that they needed to soon hang up, and that he would call her again at 7 pm the next Sunday. But before they hung up, Dawn could not help herself, and simply said to Tom, 'You know that I love you, don't you?' 'Yes,' said Tom. 'And, do you know that I too truly love you?' 'Yes,' replied Dawn, 'I know it from the deepest part of my heart.' With that both said good night and hung up. And as Dawn placed the receiver back in the holder, she was thinking about whom she could call, to tell, as Tom had advised her. She knew she could not call her parents, for they had left their cell phones at home and she did not know what country they were in at the moment. The next closest person to her would be Amy, and without thinking whether Amy might be in bed sleeping or not – and she was – Dawn had dialed the number, with the phone now ringing. After about six rings, a sleepy voice at the other end finally said, 'Hello.' Then without Amy being able to say a word, Dawn proceeded for the next ten minutes to tell her what had just happened to her. Of course, all this was very much foreign to Amy and all she could find to say, when Dawn seemed to be finished, was 'That's nice. How about I call you tomorrow night, and we can talk.' With that, she just hung up.

"Now to Him who is able to do far more abundantly beyond all that we ask or think..."

Ephesians 3:20 in part

Chapter Thirteen

/ The miracles continue

While God had been at work back at the resort, He has also been at work in Europe, although Ben and Sarah did not yet know it. They had now arrived in Rome, choosing to stay at a Bed and Breakfast whenever they can find one. Even though they likely have enough money to buy a hotel, yet at this point of their lives, they liked the simplicity of staying in a Bed and Breakfast, having found out so far that all the owners of such places had quite a life story to tell. And the same would prove to be true here in Rome also, only not with the owners, but rather with another couple who happened to stay there at the same time they did. For here they had just met Harry and Rose, an American couple, with Harry happening to a minister, in fact, a non-denominational evangelist. They were both in Rome to especially visit the Coliseum and the catacombs under the city of Rome, before heading to Israel, to conduct a Holy Land tour for a week. A group was coming in from the U.S. and Harry and his wife were to meet them at the airport in Tel Aviv in a few days.

And now Ben and Sarah make their first call back to the resort, wanting to talk to Dawn and Faith first, before calling Amy at the college. They cannot wait to tell Dawn about Paris, and the other places they have been to in France; then about Germany, with its Autobahn and its many castles; and also about Switzerland, with its beautiful mountains and so many hamlets here and there. Now they are in Rome and are about to visit that city. But the greatest news they have for Dawn is that one night, while on the Riviera in southern France, both Ben and Sarah suddenly realized that the pall, which had descended over their souls like a wet blanket since the untimely and unexpected death of their beloved Zoe, had now miraculously and suddenly lifted from them. The both of them had then repaired the breach in their marriage that this had caused, expressing the love that each knew was there for the other, but having found it next to impossible to express due to the tremendous amount of unexpressed grief each was burdened with.

Dawn listened with a tremendous sense of joy and silent uttering of thanksgiving to God as she heard this last part. She too had some great news for them, but she thought that she should show respect to her parents by letting them say all that they had to say first. Now it was her turn, first letting them know that she had spoken with Tom in Brazil. Suddenly she remembers that she forgot to ask Tom as to when he would be coming back, making a mental note to herself to ask him when he calls the following Sunday. Then she mentions to her father, with her mom listening on another phone at the Bed and Breakfast place, that after driving them to the airport she had been to the mall with Jill and picked up a Bible, which she has been reading every day since. Then because she had some questions, she had asked Tom about them when they spoke this past Sunday evening. And one thing led to another, said Dawn, so that by the end of the evening, she had come to know God in a personal relationship. When Dawn made this statement, it caused the same blank stare in her parents as it had with Amy when Dawn had called her. She was not realizing yet that her trying to explain to someone something that they had never experienced was like asking a person who had been born blind to describe a sunset, which one had never seen. And so after asking to speak to Faith for a minute or so, basically just to say 'hello,' and to let her know that they loved her, blowing kisses in the phone as they did so, Ben and Sarah both let Dawn know that they loved her and they would discuss what she had told them in greater detail once they got home. Then after saying that they would call again at the first opportunity they had, they hung up.

But what Dawn did not realize is that she had raised a number of questions in her parent's mind, when she had told them about coming to know God. This kind of language was foreign to them, and so as soon as they were off the phone with Dawn, they make their way to Harry and Rose's room at the Bed and Breakfast place. Thankfully they are not yet in bed, and the four of them sit around the round table in one corner of their room, and there spend an evening talking about God, with Ben and Sarah especially wanting to know what 'coming to know God personally' meant. To an evangelist, such a request is like honey on a saucer for a bee. Before the evening is over, Harry has realized that Ben and Dawn are not ready to know God themselves at this point, but wanting to continue to have contact with them, they make plans to visit the Coliseum and the catacombs together the next day.

The next evening, when the four of them return to the Bed and Breakfast place, after also having eaten their evening meal out before doing so, they again find themselves in Harry and Rose's room, sitting around the same table as the night before. Ben and Sarah had been astounded earlier in the day to hear all the things that Harry related to them, about what had taken place at the Coliseum and in the catacombs. The one was where untold number of Christians had died a martyrs' death, either crucified, burned alive, or fed to the lions, and even in many other forms of torture. What was especially amazing was hearing that these martyrs actually sang praises to God as they were awaiting death to come. This so perplexed onlookers in the stands that many became Christians themselves as a result, so that after a while the more the Christians were persecuted, the more they grew in number. Then in regards to the catacombs, they had learned that this had been where the Christians buried their dead, also being where they secretly met, when they had their meetings. All of this too had been foreign before to Ben and Sarah's ears. So when Harry and Rose now speak about and invite them to join the Holy Land tour, both Ben and Sarah believe this would be a great opportunity to learn more of Ancient History, and that they should take advantage of Harry's knowledge while they have the opportunity. Little did both of them realize until later, however, that God had other plans for them while in Israel.

And so, two days later, Ben and Sarah find themselves in Jerusalem, this time staying at the famous King David hotel, along with Harry, Rose, and the rest of the tour group. From there they take day trips visiting the coast to Caesarea and Mount Carmel one day, then up to the Sea of Galilee on another day, then a day up to Engedi, the Dead Sea, and the ruins of the fortress at Masada. But it is the few days spent visiting Jerusalem itself that has the greatest impact on Ben and Sarah, especially the temple Mount, the upper room, and the garden tomb. Harry had carefully explained to the group that some of these locations, apart from Masada and the temple Mount, were areas which had been determined at the time of Helena, the mother of the Emperor Constantine, who had visited the Holy Land in her day, only to identify as best as it could be done, exactly where these sites were. Harry also mentioned that the only other sure fact was that it was indeed God's own Son, Jesus Christ, Who had walked the land of Israel, during His brief thirty-three and half years on earth.

It was not surprising then, in the land where so many miracles had already taken place over two thousand years ago, that now another miracle takes place. Harry and Rose had been praying for Ben and Sarah, knowing that God was drawing them to Himself. For Harry had learnt that one evening, after the tour group had returned to the hotel, Ben and Sarah had taken a taxi and had gone to the market in the Old City, and had each bought themselves a Bible. Dawn had mentioned to them in that one conversation they had with her that she had read the accounts of Jesus' life in Matthew, Mark, Luke, and John, and now this is what they were also doing. They thought that this would be the best time to read these accounts, while in the land where these events actually took place. And they were right. As they visited these places, they became alive to Ben and Sarah.

But then too, God was at work here. Therefore, it was not a coincidence that on the last night of the tour, while Ben and Sarah are with Harry and Rose in their hotel room, that they too hear the message of salvation, namely that God's precious Son, Jesus Christ, came from Heaven to earth, to take on a body like ours, in the innocence of Adam and born of a virgin, to live a sinless life for thirty-three and half years, and then being given into the hand of sinners in the will of His Father, to die on a cross to pay a debt He did not owe on a behalf of a sinful human race, before being raised from the dead the third day. When Ben and Sarah both call on God silently, as Dawn had done, they too receive the forgiveness of sins and eternal life with God. Now it was their turn to call someone dear to them, and tell them the good news of what had just happened to them.

This time, it was Dawn's turn to be woken up in the middle of the night. She was surprised and overjoyed at the same time in hearing the news. What a gift from God she had received, and now her parents had also received. Her parents said that they would be home this Sunday at 2 pm, arriving from Tel Aviv, and they asked Dawn if she would pick them up, with little Faith there as well, of course. Dawn remembered Tom's call the previous Sunday evening, where he had told her that he would be home in ten days, which was a Wednesday, and had asked Dawn if she would pick him up at the airport. The doctors had finally discovered what the Project Manager had, which was not malaria, but rather some type of infection, which they were now treating, so successfully in fact that he had been discharged from the hospital and was now recuperating in his temporary quarters on site. Dawn also related this news to her parents.

And then when her parents had exhausted themselves talking, in the same excitement she had felt not that long ago, they said their goodbyes and hung up. What Dawn would not know until later is that her parents then called Amy at college, not wanting to wait until later before calling her, to tell her the news of their salvation. But poor Amy, twice in the space of less than two weeks she had now been woken up in the middle of the night, and both times with the same kind of news, about a subject she knew nothing about, but which she was now determined to find out more about. So a few days later, while Amy was looking up some information on a bulletin board near the main office, she happened – and again we need to remember that there are no coincidences with God – to notice a poster posted by a Christian group on campus, announcing when they would be meeting again and where, which Amy noted, for now she was planning to attend this meeting and find out about what it was that members of her family were getting involved with, and with such excitement that they felt the need to call her even in the middle of the night!

"Commit your works to the Lord and your plans will be established."

Proverbs 16:3

Chapter Fourteen

/ Dawn meets Tom's family

That Thanksgiving at the house was a memorable one. None of them, except Tom, really knew the true meaning of Thanksgiving before. They just knew that it was a holiday, never having really connected with those pilgrims from England and other countries, who had made the transatlantic voyage to a new land in order to avoid being persecuted to death for their faith in The One true God. When they had disembarked, they had knelt together on this soil and given thanks to God. Now Ben's family and invited guests were holding hands around the dining room table at the resort, being this time led in prayer by Ben, before partaking of a turkey dinner together. Tom was there, as was Dawn and Faith, of course Ben and Sarah. But Amy was also there, having brought a male friend from college with her, one she had met in the Christian group that she had now joined.

So when the meal was over, and everyone had made their way to the living room to relax, Amy, with her friend standing beside her at the entrance to the living room, says that she has an announcement to make. The words are not yet off her lips and the thought which immediately springs to everyone's mind is that she is either pregnant, or is getting married, or both. So what a surprise when she discloses that she too has come to personal faith in God, with her friend here having led her to Christ. Then without hesitation, as if on cue in a movie, all of them get up from their chairs, sofa, and comfort chairs, and surround Amy, giving her hugs and kisses, also shaking hands with the young man, Robert, and thanking him. Then Ben does what a father does best, while they are standing there, he leads his family in another prayer of thanksgiving! The only perplexed one this time is little Faith. She just sits on her plastic three wheeler and grins, from ear to ear. And no doubt joined in Heaven by a host of angels.

Later that evening, as Tom and Dawn take a stroll on their property around the house, he too has news to share with her. After returning to the office from Brazil, the partners of the firm had received a glowing report from the main contractor building the hydroelectric project, saying that Tom had performed well in replacing the Project Manager, while he had been absent due to sickness. Tom, he said, had solved all the problems that they had encountered. And now the partners had decided to make Tom a Supervisor in the office, with a view to making him a Project Manager in the near future. Dawn is happy for Tom, as can be expected, but at the same time, she knows that if Tom remains with the firm, eventually he too will likely be sent to some far away place, for a year or more on some project. Somehow, she has trouble being happy about such a prospect, so secretly starts to pray for Tom to find some other line of work. Little does she know that God is also at work in that area and has a surprise in store for them.

Then before they head back to the house and Tom leaves for his unit, he has something to ask Dawn. When he says this, Dawn's heart skips a beat, with the one thought coming to her mind at the moment being to start to wonder whether he is about to propose to her? But before her thoughts can get away on her, Tom mentions that he would like Dawn to fly with him to his hometown, to meet his parents, at the earliest opportunity. He says he has not seen them for quite a few months, actually since before meeting Dawn, although they know all about her from Tom having told them in his occasional phone calls. Dawn ponders this for a moment and realizes that now she can indeed leave the resort for a few days, since her father has again resumed his duties at chief executive of The Twin Peaks Resort, Golf, and RV Park. He no longer drinks and his mother is no longer hooked on prescription drugs, which means that her life has returned to normal on the home front. So she turns to Tom and gives him a big hug, letting him know that she is proud of him in regards to his promotion, and also that she will gladly go with him to meet his parents. And then both of them think of Faith at the same time, and agree that she should come along also. After all, she is part of Dawn. How can Tom's family meet Dawn without Faith being there also, they both conclude.

As they reach the front door to the house, Tom again takes Dawn in his arms, holding her for a long time, again letting her know that he loves her, to which she responds that she does also. It is on nights like this, and also when she picked him up at the airport, that he would like to kiss her, but they have already made the decision together that they would not kiss until their wedding night, knowing full well what a kiss can lead to, especially when two people love each other. So with this Tom starts his walk back to his unit, while Dawn makes her way to the living room, where everyone still is, to tell them about Tom's promotion, and also that she has been invited to go with him to visit his family. Her mother asks 'when,' but Dawn replies that she does not yet know, as Tom wants to contact his parents first and see when it would be most convenient for them. And with that, Dawn picks up Faith from her father's lap and asks her to say 'nighty, nighty' to everyone because it is now her bedtime. After having changed Faith into her pajamas, and read a couple of stories from the Toddler's Bible, Dawn tucks her in and kisses her, before making her way to her own bedroom. Now her thoughts are fully on meeting Tom's family. What this also means, she realizes, is that at some point in the near future Tom is going to propose to her, obviously not wanting to do so before meeting his parents. So with these pleasant thoughts circling around in her head, Dawn has one of the best sleeps she has ever had.

The flight over to Tom's parents is a pleasant one, taking about two hours of flying time. Dawn had expected Faith to possibly be scared, of the height and the noise, but she just slept most of the way. Tom's parents are both at the airport now to meet them, for they live about an hour from the airport and there is no airport where they live. As they make their way in the airport to the baggage area, Dawn cannot help noticing all the blacks that she sees. They are everywhere. In fact, there are just as many blacks as there are whites. She ponders this for a moment and then remembers that this state is part of what is known as 'the Bible belt,' which is a good thing, in terms of no doubt having some positive effect on race relations.

When they pick up their luggage and make their way to the arrivals area, Dawn is hugged by both Bill and Harriet, as she is introduced to them. As she sees Tom's parents, she now knows where Tom gets his good looks from. Then all attention focuses on little Faith. Bill and Harriet's three children, two boys and a girl, are all around Tom's age, he being the oldest, with none of them married, and so it has been awhile since they have been able to hold a young one. And Harriet is typical of many woman, she especially dotes over Faith, being unable to contain her amazement at how pretty she is, but then in having now seen Dawn, she also remarks 'like mother like daughter.' They quickly load into Bill's car and make their way towards the acreage they live on.

Tom uses the three days that they are there to drive Dawn around, to see the nearest town, where they normally buy their supplies and also where he went to school in the early years. Dawn is introduced to many of Tom's friends who have not left the area, as they later sit in a coffee shop and chat. Dawn tells Tom that she really likes her folks, and also his younger brother Gerry and sister Chloe. They both realize once again, as they sit there and talk about whatever comes to their mind, just how comfortable they are in each other's company. Like a well-fitting glove, which is always the case when God brings two people together. Harriet is also a good cook, like Dawn's own mother, and as Dawn thinks of this as she sits there, this makes her realize that one of the skills she needs to work on is her cooking. Obviously Tom was brought up on good meals and he will no doubt be looking for the same from her if they marry, as she expects will happen some day soon. The thing is she has been busy doing the job that her father was supposed to be doing for over two years, and has not had much time for cooking meals. Being well-off financially, they have been able to hire whatever help has ever been needed. But still, Dawn does not want to have to rely on outside help, she determines, she simply needs to work on her cooking skills once she gets back home, now that her father has resumed his proper duties. And besides, she concludes to herself, it will be nice to spend time in the kitchen with her mother, Sarah. She knows she is very close to her father, especially since they worked together for over six months just before her pregnancy. Now it will be nice to spend time with her mother, Sarah, for a change.

Before they leave the parent's home to return to the resort, Tom has talked to his parents in private and has told them that he plans to talk to Dawn's father, Ben, when they get back, in order to ask him for Dawn's hand in marriage. And now he has asked his parents to throw a little BBQ the evening before they leave for the purpose of inviting over those friends he is planning to invite to the wedding, so that they would all have an opportunity to meet Dawn before the wedding. But he does not want Dawn to know that this is why they will all be there. And so, when they do have the get together, Dawn suspects nothing, thinking only that these are more of Tom's friends like the ones she met at the coffee shop. What Dawn also does not know is that Tom plans to ask two of these friends to be part of the wedding party, along with his brother Gerry, plus a friend from the firm he is now at, plus his roommate from college, whom he roomed with for four years, to be his best man. Tom is planning all these things now, including mentioning to his sister in private before he leaves that he will later suggest to Dawn that she be asked to be in the wedding party. And so, while Dawn thought that the purpose of the trip was simply to meet Tom's family, yet Tom had many other purposes in mind, which he could not yet share with her.

When Tom drives Dawn and Faith back to the resort from the airport the next morning, he is invited by Ben to come and join them for supper that evening. Tom readily agrees, for he does want to see Ben in private at some point soon, and thinks that this might just be the occasion he is looking for. So while Dawn spends the afternoon telling Ben and Sarah about her trip, Tom returns to his unit and spends time in prayer, after unpacking. He knows that God has been bringing him and Dawn together, but he still needs God's mind as to when to get married and so forth. In other words, he does not want to leave God out of the planning.

After the meal that evening, Tom takes Ben aside and mentions that he would like to talk to him in private, if he could, and if possible, without Dawn suspecting anything. Ben realizes what Tom might want to talk about, and so he walks to the kitchen, where Sarah and Dawn are at the moment, and mentions that he and Tom are going to his office for a while. And with that he leaves, with Tom behind him. When they get to Ben's office at the end of long hallway on the main floor, Ben closes the door behind Tom to ensure that they are not disturbed. Ben makes his way to the plush leather chairs at one end of the office and sits down, motioning to Tom to sit down in the other one. Then Ben looks at Tom, as if to say, for him to tell him what is on his mind. And at this point Tom is really glad that Ben is now a Christian, for it makes his task a lot easier, since now he is not just talking with Dawn's father, but also a brother, who is also part of the one family of God. With this in mind, Tom shares with Ben that he loves Dawn and has loved her from the moment they first met. And with this he does not beat around the bush and comes right to the point and asks Ben for his daughter's hand in marriage. All this was new to Ben, in terms of the one being asked, instead of the one doing the asking, and he simply extends his hand to Tom and while holding it says to him that he does not know a better man than he that he would rather give his daughter to. And spontaneously, both men rise and hug each other.

Then when they are seated again, Ben asks Tom about his plans, as to when he wants to ask Dawn and what date he has in mind for the wedding. Tom says that he has another request of him, which is that Ben invite all of his family to the resort for New Years and that while both families are here, he would ask Dawn in marriage. That would also give both families an opportunity to meet each other, says Tom. Ben agrees fully and adds that he will be paying for their trip back and forth, and look after all their needs while here at the resort, having heard from Dawn already that Tom's family is not rich like theirs. Then the only other request Tom has for Ben is to have an alcohol-free wedding, with even the toasts being with carbonated grape juice. Since his recent bout with alcoholism, Ben heartily agrees. Then as they were about to leave the office, Tom mentions that as to the date, which both had forgotten to talk about, would be Saturday, May 20th, but that this would be subject to change since he had not yet talked to Dawn about it, of course, and she needed to have an input into this. And with these things in mind, both men rejoin the women in the living room, where they both get stares as they walk in the room, as if to say, 'what have you men been discussing,' but both Sarah and Dawn suspecting what it might have been say nothing more.

The next month is hectic for Tom. He has contacted his parents and they have agreed to come, being glad that they will not have any expenses to pay, but also glad to have the opportunity to meet the rest of Dawn's family, having heard that they are now all believers in God. He also wants to talk to the partners at the firm in private, to tell them of his plans for next May, to ensure they do not plan to send him somewhere on a project. Tom also needs to find an engagement ring for Dawn. He is glad that although Dawn's family is wealthy, they have never looked at wealth as a symbol of being better than anyone else. In other words, they have managed to remain down to earth folks with simple tastes despite having money to burn. Tom is glad of this, as it makes his task of choosing a ring for Dawn that much easier. And he was glad when Ben called him on his cell phone to tell him that he shared all their talk with his own father, Jim, on the phone, and invited him to be at the resort also at New Years, so that he and Dot could also be there when the announcement is made. Both had forgotten about Jim and Dot, and so Tom is glad that Ben has now invited them. He and Jim had hit if off well the first and only time they had met the day the casino project was publicly announced.

"…a man shall leave his father and his mother, and be joined to his wife; and they shall become one flesh."

Genesis 2:24 in part

Chapter Fifteen

/ Wedding bells are a ringing

When Dawn hears from Tom just one week before Christmas that his parents will be coming to the resort to meet her parents the following week, her heart skips a beat. She has been suspecting since they returned from meeting his parents that Tom might be planning to ask her to marry him, either at Christmas or New Years. Now she knows that it will definitely not be at Christmas. She has been dreaming about being married since a little girl, and now she realizes that her dream is about to come true. Ben has already shared with Sarah all he and Tom talked about that night, including inviting Tom's family to the resort. Sarah is really glad of all she hears, and mentions to Ben how fortunate they both need to be for not being in the same state now as they had been just a few months ago. What a difference their lives now were since becoming Christians, and all for the better. The peace and the joy they were now experiencing in walking with God together, which they had never known before. And Amy too, now being a believer also. What a wonderful work God had done in their family, they both thought.

Tom is more than happy to return the favor and now pick up his family at the airport. Ben has lent him one of the two resort vehicles that they use to shuttle guests to and from the city. This is the first time Tom's family has been to this part of the country, and they especially marvel at the mountains in the distance as they drive toward the resort. Jim and Dot have already arrived, and also Amy and Robert, who are now fairly serious in their relationship. The casino is now nearing completion, and Jim and Dot are glad to be back to take a look at their house, which is under construction near the casino. Jim has decided to move back to this area, since he will be the managing partner of the casino. The casino needed only 50 acres and they bought 260 acres, leaving a 60 acre parcel for future expansion, with Jim and Dot living on the other 150 acres, where the house was being built. There were still cattle grazing on the remaining portion, which Jim planned to keep for the time being. He has hired a Project Manager to oversee the construction of the casino on a day to day basis, and it will now be good to check in with him in person, instead of just talking on the phone daily, as they have been doing.

Tom had been thinking of how he would ask Dawn in marriage and when, wanting it to be somewhat of a surprise in the way it was done, even though everyone was anticipating it. And so he had contracted a Company, which did this type of thing, to fly past the resort at 2 pm on the day before New Years, with a banner reading, 'Dawn, I love you. Will you marry me, Tom.' This plan had also been related to Ben and Tom's father, so that all could be outside at the time, while Tom went on a walk with Dawn to the lake. And so, after lunch, while Tom and Dawn are now at the lake, looking out over the waveless water, they suddenly hear an airplane in the sky and both instinctively look up. Dawn had wondered when Tom might propose, but she certainly had not expected this. As soon as she looked up and read the banner flying in the wind, which anyone and everyone who was outside and looking up could read, she burst into tears and threw herself into Tom's open arms to receive her. Through her sobs of joy, she lets him know that she indeed would be happy to marry him, letting him also know that there is no other man on earth that she would rather spend her life with. After the longest of time in each other's arms, they now both make their way back to the house, with Tom having told Dawn that the whole family would know already, since he had told them about the banner. And so, when they reach the house, Tom leads Dawn to the pool area, where he anticipates everyone being. Everyone rise as one to surround the happy couple and hug and kiss them, letting them know just how happy they are for them. Faith is again taking in all this and no doubt wondering to herself what these funny adults are all up to this time! When Tom and Dawn have a moment alone later that night, after ringing in the New Year and before Tom retires to his unit, they both decide that May 20th would indeed be a good date to have the wedding.

Now that the date had been set, it suddenly dawns on the two love birds that there is just a little over four and half months until the wedding, and so much to plan. Therefore, to say that things were hectic in the next few weeks and months would be an understatement. As decisions are made by Tom and Dawn each evening, they are implemented by Dawn and her mother during the day. And with God superintending over the whole affair, as this is a work of His in progress, then all fell into place, like a modular home being put together on site. There would be five bridesmaid and five groomsmen. Dawn had trouble finding five, since she had been so busy with the business and raising Faith in the last two years, that she did not have much time to think about cultivating friendships. But she finally settled on Jill as her maid of honor, then Amy, then Tom's sister Chloe; then the office secretary, who had been doing all her official correspondence the last two years, so that a friendship had developed. Then as a fifth she picked one of the maids, who had worked at the house for about four years and whom Dawn had also developed a friendship with.

It had also been agreed that the wedding would take place in the large area between the pool and the fence at the house, which were all manicured lawns. They would get married at 11 am, with Tom's senior minister at his church officiating. The meal would be catered by their own two restaurants at the resort, with each preparing part of the food. There was not to be a dance, but an orchestra was hired to play during the wedding ceremony, during the meal, and as the guests relaxed with non-alcoholic punch after the speeches later in the afternoon. Tom had reserved a room in the Tower Inn in the city for his wedding night. It had a large balcony overlooking the city, where they could enjoy breakfast together the morning following the wedding, before attending church where Tom had been worshipping, Then they would be returning to the house for a 2 pm lunch, where all were again invited to attend, as gifts were to be opened. Then Tom and Dawn were to fly off to the Bahamas for a week, where Ben had a friend with a resort there, who when he found out Ben's daughter was getting married, had offered to put them up at no cost for the week. Ben's parents were paying for the flights as part of their wedding gift to them.

We have no doubt all heard the saying that 'April showers brings May flowers.' Well, what is also true is that God has so designed spring as the time of year when the earth is renewed. Most creatures have their young in the spring and all of that which died off in the fall, suddenly blooms to new life at this time of year. Therefore, when the day arrives for Tom and Dawn's wedding, it is with the promise of new life starting. Not only two lives becoming one, but also becoming one in order as to produce offspring some day out of their love union. And so May 20th that year, which was a Saturday, could not have been more perfect, as if one were reading a fairy tale. Tom was glad to be living in an area where there was on average 210 days of sunshine a year.

All the plans which they have made prove to have been the right choices, as everything goes on cue, as if this was a movie in progress, or even a story as part of a work of fiction. Dawn had looked so beautiful in walking down the 'aisle' that Tom had tears flowing freely down his face when Dawn finally reached him, being escorted proudly by a beaming Ben. Then the meal was great, and the speeches, well, let us just say there was much laughter. Harry and Rose, were there, as surprise guests, Dawn finally getting to meet the couple which led her parents to faith in God back in the King David Hotel in Jerusalem. Little did she know that this man was to play a large role in their lives in the days to come. Then before they know it, it is time for Tom and Dawn to leave for the city. Tom has reservations at 7 pm in a revolving restaurant in the city, which is in the same Tower Inn as where they will be spending the night. This way the two lovers have an opportunity to unwind before jumping in the standup Jacuzzi in their bedroom, to unwind further, before tasting more of each other's lips, now that they have had their first kiss at the wedding ceremony that afternoon.

Later, as Tom holds Dawn in his arms, as they both lie naked on the bed, he whispers a prayer to God in her hearing, asking God to make him the husband which Dawn needs and also asking that he always be enabled to meet Dawn's every need, before looking after his own. When Dawn hears this, her heart melts and she feels drawn even closer to Tom. Then when their yearning bodies finally come together in that most intimate of acts, which God has designed for married couples to enjoy, she realizes for the first time that all she had ever experienced before was not love, but rather lust. Both are four letter words, but what a world of difference! She also now realizes, as Tom moves in and out of her, that when God is in something, like He was

110

now in this lovemaking, then it was surreal. In other words, this was now blessed of God, Who had given His approval, so that instead of having guilt feelings, as she had experienced every time she had sex with Dave, now there was nothing but a wave after wave of good feelings flooding over her. Even though Tom orgasms prematurely, due to his being overexcited - and also Dawn just finding out he was a virgin - did not spoil the occasion. Since it was fairly early, neither one was yet sleepy, so Tom remained implanted in Dawn so that after a few minutes he was hard again, and this time Dawn took great pleasure in the mutual orgasm they had together. Then as the two lovers held each other, they both fell asleep without realizing it.

The sun was still shining brightly when they gathered at the house the next afternoon to have lunch and open gifts, with most of the same guests being there. And now Tom and Dawn were to have the surprise of their life. Dawn's grandfather had not made any speeches the night before, because without anyone knowing about this except his wife Dot, he was planning to make one this afternoon as part of an important announcement. So by 4 pm, when all the other gifts had been opened, Jim got up and started his speech. He said that he had always loved his granddaughter, who was now married, and who had also given him and his wife great joy in a great granddaughter. And now he wanted to do something for her, since she was there when the resort needed her the most. He went on and said that he and his wife Dot were now giving her and Tom their 49% share of the resort. The casino was now open and doing so well, he said, so that he had more money than he knew what to do with.

At that moment he sat down and there were loud gasps from all those in attendance, who could grasp the significance of this move. For what it meant is that both Tom and Dawn would now be instant multi-millionaires many times over, and would not have to work for a living, but could pursue any dreams they wished to pursue. With Tom and Dawn sitting on the plane holding hands later that evening, each of them lost in thought, wondering if they had been dreaming all this and at any moment they would wake up and all would vanish like a puff of smoke. Then as the plane landed in the Bahamas, they knew without a doubt that this was real. And with thankful hearts to God, they began their honeymoon.

"And we know that God causes all things to work together for good to those who love God, to those who are called according to His purpose."

Romans 8:28

Chapter Sixteen

/ Planned and unplanned

As Tom and Dawn fly back from the Bahamas, they have now made a big decision together. Before their honeymoon, they were planning to live at Dawn's house for the time being, since that was a familiar place for Faith, and it was also the only home Dawn had ever known. Besides, Tom's rental unit was coming up for renewal in a month, and they obviously could not live there, as it was too small. Now that they owned 49% of the resort, they had many options to consider, which they did in all the hours they had to talk together, when they were not being intimate. Dawn thought sex was pleasurable in her earlier years, but now she was seeing it as really one of God's great gifts to humanity, but which is only great within the context which God designed it for, which is marriage. In other words, sexual relations outside of marriage is sex. Sexual relations within marriage is love making of the highest degree, for it has God's blessing, and with His blessing comes the peace and the joy in the midst of two persons becoming one.

And so, by the time Tom and Dawn embark on the plane to take them home, they have made the decision to buy the 3,000 acre cattle ranch which Dawn's grandfather had told them about when they talked after the opening of gifts. He had said that he had this ranch in view before, at the time he was looking for land for the casino. But since it was not near the Interstate, then he had let it go, but had liked it. Tom and Dawn had taken a quick drive by on their way to the airport and had downloaded information on it while on their honeymoon. It was not far from Ben and Sarah's house, being just down the road going north past the single units and the RV Park.

When that decision was reached the day before they left the Bahamas, Dawn shares with Tom that this is also an answer to prayer. And then she explains to Tom that the night he shared about his promotion, she was afraid that at some point in the future, Tom might become a Project Manager on some far away project, which would take him away from the family for a long time. Tom thought about this for a moment and realizes that what Dawn just said was true. That is exactly what was likely to happen. Therefore, as they discuss their future plans further, another decision which they arrive at is that Tom should resign his position with the consulting firm he is with. When Tom prays about this before bedtime that night, he senses in his spirit that it is the right thing to do. And now they are heading back with big steps to take.

As Dawn and Tom reach the house, both are very much looking forward to see little Faith, who was being watched over by grandpa and grandma while they were away on their honeymoon. They cannot wait to tell Ben and Sarah about their plans of buying a cattle ranch, not knowing that while they were away, there were a lot of plans going on at the resort, as well. Harry, the evangelist, and his wife Rose, who had been Ben and Sarah's guests at Dawn's wedding, are still at the house when Tom and Dawn arrive. While they all sit around the pool, sipping lemonade during the afternoon, Dawn's parents listen approvingly as they hear Tom and Dawn talk excitedly about their plans to buy the cattle ranch, also letting them know about Tom leaving his present employment. When they are finished, it is Ben and Sarah's turn. While they had been in Rome, and later in Israel together, it had never been disclosed by Rose that she too was a nurse, same as Sarah. And now Sarah would like to expand the clinic. She wants to advertise for an MD to come and start a family practice there, with both Sarah and Rose also working at the clinic, with Sarah being the Clinic Manager. And since Harry would now be living there, then Ben has suggested that they build a Mission House next to the expanded clinic, where Harry and Rose could stay, with there also being a large meeting area, which could be used for services, meetings, and as a dining area.

As Tom and Dawn retire to Dawn's bedroom later that evening, they look at each other in utter amazement at all the changes which God is bringing about in their lives, and that of Ben and Sarah, and all for the better. But little does either one of them know that there are even more changes coming. With Jim and Dot now living just down the road across the Interstate, there are now fairly frequent family gatherings. And at such a gathering, a few months after Tom and Dawn's return from their honeymoon, Jim mentions that the casino, which is now open, buys a lot of food from the city every second day. When he says this, Ben realizes that both restaurants at the resort do also, as does their store on site. And when both Ben and his father think about this further, they both come to the same conclusion at the same time, which is: Why not grow a lot of their own food right where they are, for the casino, the two restaurants, and the store? It is as if they struck a match in a gunpowder room, for now everyone jumps into the conversation at once, with ideas flying in every which direction. After all, they now have two cattle ranches, one small and one fairly large, which can supply all the beef that they would ever need. But what about the fruit and vegetables? They would have to buy more land to grow that, but since they live in a semi-arid area, the soil is not that great for crops, being better suited for grazing, which is why there are so many cattle ranches in the area. And so this is where the conversation stops when each couple disperse to their own homes that evening. But plans are made to discuss this further at Jim's house in a few days, where the three couples, plus Faith will be.

In the meantime, Tom, as a Project Engineer, has his thinking cap on, and over supper at their ranch one evening a couple of days later, shares with Dawn a plan that he has. He mentions that once a week for many years, the resort has had to hire trucks to empty the septic tanks at the many buildings at the resort and take that sewage back to the nearest sewage treatment plant in the city. When the casino was opened, they built their own small sewage treatment plant, but large enough to handle a future expansion. The treated water from this plant was then going into the river flowing nearby. Why not buy our own trucks here for the resort, said Tom, and truck the sewage from the septic tanks to the plant at the casino, and pay them a fee for handling it, which could be the same fee as they now pay to the city. And instead of having the waste water go into the river, they could use the remaining acres of Jim's ranch and irrigate it with this water and grow all the fruits and vegetables that they would need at both the casino and the resort. When Dawn hears of it, she is ecstatic. She now realizes what she had thought when she interviewed Tom that day a year and a half ago, which was that Tom would be an asset to the resort. Now that was being realized. There was only one problem, said Tom. Those who owned the resort were now all Christians, but Jim and his partners, who owned the casino, were not. And Tom remembered God's warning that believers should never be partners with unbelievers, neither in marriage nor in business. So until the next family meeting, Tom and Dawn decide to make this a matter for prayer, asking God to give them the wisdom to know what to do. Then as would happen, the next meeting was close to Thanksgiving, so all agree that they should have their get together that same weekend.

Amy and Robert, who are very serious in their relationship now, arrive on the Friday evening, and in a private moment with Ben, Robert asks him for Amy's hand in marriage, with a wedding planned for the following summer, after both graduate. Ben likes Robert and knows him to be a Christian, in fact remembering that he was the one to lead his daughter to faith in God. Ben says to him what he had said to Tom before, that he did not know a better man than him to give his daughter to. And with that, the two men shake hands and hug, as father-in-law and son-in-law to be. So the next evening, without any fanfare, Robert proposes to Amy. She too had anticipated this moment, just not knowing the exact moment that it would come, thinking perhaps that it might be at Christmas or New Years, at least before graduation. And so when they have their Thanksgiving meal the next evening, this announcement by Amy and Robert is the talk of the evening.

Then the three couples excuse themselves and go to Ben's office in the other part of the house to have their meeting, leaving Faith with Amy and Robert in the living room. Tom has already told Ben about the plans that he had thought of, including not knowing how to handle the problem of being unequally yoked with Jim in the proposed venture. So when they are together, Ben lets Tom make his proposal to the others, and when Tom is finished, he adds as sensitively as he can, that there is only one problem. Jim, who thinks this is just a super idea, asks what that might be. Ben opens a Bible on his desk and turns to the passage where God says this and reads it aloud. And although Jim is not yet a believer, he understands right away what the situation is here. And he now sits down and ponders this for a few minutes, then speaks with Dot without being heard by the others. Both Ben and Tom, including Sarah and Dawn, are hoping that neither Jim nor Dot will be offended. But to their surprise, Jim says that he and Dot fully understand the predicament and wish to honor God's word. So since Amy is about to be married, he will have his land subdivided, keeping only the portion for future casino expansion and a few acres that their new house is on. Then as a wedding gift, he and Dot will give the remaining land over to Amy and Robert, where the crops are all proposed to be grown on, not charging for the waste water going to the farm to be, since it is only going there instead of the river. Jim and Dot will also build Amy and Robert a large house on the land, so that they can live there. And since Amy and Robert are both Christians, then that solves the problem. When the others here of this plan, they are delighted beyond belief, realizing within themselves that God was definitely at work here, to solve a problem which seemed insurmountable to them. When the three couple conclude their meeting a few minutes later, Jim relates their plan to Amy and Robert, including what had been decided this evening. Both Amy and Robert are overwhelmed with emotion, not knowing how to thank everyone. They then share with the group that both of them had been unsure of what to do after graduation, or where to go, but one thought both had expressed is that it would take them close to the resort area. Now what had been just a thought was about to become a reality.

At their next family meeting a week later, when one thinks there cannot possibly be anything more which can happen in their lives at the moment, Dawn announces that she is six weeks pregnant. She and Tom was at their doctor in the city a couple of days ago, and he had confirmed it. Now what a difference this announcement was compared to almost three years ago, when Dawn had to let her family know that she was pregnant. She was now likewise to have a baby, but the circumstances were now totally different. Instead of having a man who did not love her or want her, now she had one who did. Before she was not married, with God having designed marriage specifically as the breeding ground for having and raising offspring, now she fitted in that plan, being married this time around. As Tom and Dawn took a leisurely walk after the evening meal, and before their meeting, they stood outside looking at the sun starting to set over the mountains to the West. Dawn, who was now reading her Bible each morning upon waking, with a time of prayer, related to Tom what she had read that morning in God's word, "'For I know the plans that I have for you,' declares the Lord, 'plans for welfare and not for calamity to give you a future and a hope." As Dawn and Tom thought about this verse of Scripture, they could not hold back from both expressing just how good God had been to both of them, and how together they looked forward to what God had in store for them in the future. All they could say was: To God be the glory, the praise, and the thanksgiving, both now and forevermore! Amen.

"   "for those who honor Me I will honor…"

1 Samuel 2:30 in part

The next book

God has given His approval to two new books, the one being titled, "Father, Forgive Them..." The author's third book deals with the fact that the end of the present age is very close. This book picks up from there and will examine WHY God's judgment will fall on this present world. In other words, when God's judgment comes, and we can be absolutely sure that it is coming, then no one of all mankind facing that judgment will be able to say that it was not justified. All throughout history, God has destroyed one nation after another due to the sins of those nations. This was meant as a history lesson for those nations which come afterwards. In this book, we will also examine this history lesson from God and apply it to our own day. This is a book you will not want to miss, if you are concerned about the current events in the world and are wondering what this world is coming to! This will be the author's eighth book in the Truth Seeker's Library™ series.

The second book God has given His approval to is a sequel to the present book and is titled, "Dawn Meets Glory." This will be the author's second book in a series called, "The Christian Fiction Library™ series. This book continues the story of Dawn and Tom, Ben and Sarah, and many old and new characters. As with the first book, this is written from a Christian worldview and has interesting insights drawn from the author's counseling ministry, which may be of help to many readers. This book series also seeks to portray the Christian life as God intends it to be lived.

Made in the USA
Charleston, SC
13 February 2015